More Adventures of the
Plant That Ate Dirty Socks

Other Avon Camelot Books by
Nancy McArthur

THE PLANT THAT ATE DIRTY SOCKS
THE RETURN OF THE PLANT THAT ATE DIRTY SOCKS
THE ESCAPE OF THE PLANT THAT ATE DIRTY SOCKS
THE SECRET OF THE PLANT THAT ATE DIRTY SOCKS

NANCY McARTHUR lives in Berea, Ohio, a suburb of Cleveland. In addition to writing books, she teaches journalism part-time at Baldwin-Wallace College and speaks to school groups. "I start writing with a very messy rough draft," she says, "and revise at least two or three times." *More Adventures of the Plant That Ate Dirty Socks* is the fifth book about Michael and Norman and their amazing plants. The sixth one will be published in July, 1995. Ms. McArthur's shorter books are *The Adventure of the Backyard Sleepout, The Adventure of the Buried Treasure, Megan Gets a Dollhouse,* and *Pickled Peppers.*

More Adventures of the

Plant That Ate Dirty Socks

Nancy McArthur

AN AVON CAMELOT BOOK

MORE ADVENTURES OF THE PLANT THAT ATE DIRTY SOCKS is an original publication of Avon Books. This work has never before appeared in book form. Any similarity to actual persons or events is purely coincidental.

AVON BOOKS
A division of
The Hearst Corporation
1350 Avenue of the Americas
New York, New York 10019

Copyright © 1994 by Nancy McArthur
Published by arrangement with the author
Library of Congress Catalog Card Number: 94-94095
ISBN: 0-380-77663-4
RL: 5.3

First Avon Camelot Printing: October 1994

CAMELOT TRADEMARK REG. U.S. PAT. OFF. AND IN OTHER COUNTRIES, MARCA REGISTRADA, HECHO EN U.S.A.

Printed in the U.S.A.

OPM 10 9 8 7 6 5 4 3 2

In memory of my mother and father
IRENE P. McARTHUR
RUSSELL McARTHUR
with love and gratitude

Thanks to: Barbara McArthur; Susan McArthur; John McArthur; Ellen Krieger; Tina Moore of the Blue Marble bookstore in Ft. Thomas, Kentucky; Helen Rathburn; Baya Sommers Watson; Nick Stiner Riley; Emma Stiner Riley; Margaret Stiner; Sue Coates; Sue Norton; Grayson Lappert.

Chapter 1

"Put your right vine in," sang the irritating voice. "Take your right vine out—no, wait! That's not your right vine!"

Michael snuggled deeper into his pillow. He didn't have to open even one eye to figure out what was happening. His younger brother, Norman, the expert pest and neatness nut, was teaching his giant pet plant, Fluffy, to do the Hokey Pokey.

Norman sang on, "Put your right vine in and shake it all about!"

A mass of leaves twitched all over Michael's face. That startled him completely awake. It was his own plant, Stanley, standing next to Michael's bed, trying to do the Hokey Pokey, too.

Michael brushed the leaves away from his mouth. "Cut out the Hokey Pokeying!" he snarled at Norman. "I'm trying to sleep! And don't teach my plant anything! Stick to your own plant!"

Norman replied huffily, "I wasn't teaching Stanley. He was copying what I was teaching Fluffy!"

Michael pulled his blanket over his head. He liked to sleep late on Saturdays, but Norman always did something to wake him up.

Michael mumbled, "Go teach Fluffy in the living room. Stanley and I want to sleep without you bothering us."

"I'm not bothering Stanley," said Norman. "He wants to dance along with Fluffy."

Michael sat up. "Don't teach them any new stuff that could cause more messy disasters. Not after all we went through to get Mom and Dad to let us keep the plants!"

Norman replied, "Dancing isn't messy! And the Hokey Pokey is not a disaster!"

Michael looked at the floor next to his bed to see if Stanley had eaten all six dirty socks he had put out for his plant's late-night meal. There were no leftovers.

The six-foot-tall plants didn't do much during the day, but at night they did amazing things. Their pots were firmly fastened to skateboards so the family could roll them to wherever they needed to be put. But the plants used their vines to pull themselves around on their own.

While the boys slept, the plants picked up socks

with their vines and lifted them to rolled-up leaves that looked like green ice-cream cones. These sucked in the socks with a loud "schlurrrrp!" Then, the plants burped. Fluffy also made a noise that sounded like "ex" because Norman had tried to teach him to say "excuse me."

Last summer, Michael had figured out how to get both plants to eat fewer socks by putting them outside all day to get more sun. That way they made more of their own food inside themselves by photosynthesis. But when the weather got cold, the plants had to stay indoors. With only a few hours of sun from the window between the boys' beds, they went back to eating more socks.

Now Michael had to wear three pairs a day to have enough dirty ones for Stanley each night. Sometimes, he wore two pairs at a time. That made his feet so thick that they didn't fit in his shoes. So he only did that when he was staying home. He also wore socks to bed to get a head start on preparing the next night's dinner for Stanley.

Norman didn't have this problem because Fluffy ate only clean socks.

Since buying so many socks was expensive, Mom and Dad were thinking about building a small greenhouse on the back of their home. That way the plants could get sun all day, year-round. They'd been looking at greenhouses in catalogs to see what kinds they could afford.

In the kitchen Mom was talking on the phone. Michael dumped a heap of his favorite cereal, Super Gooper Bunch-O-Crunch, into his bowl. Flakes spilled over the rim. He sloshed milk on, splashing his placemat and his pajama top.

Norman poured a neat mound of his favorite, Tummy Yummy Globsters. He carefully added milk.

When Mom hung up, Dad asked, "What was that all about?"

She replied, "That was Susan Sparks. She invited us to visit them the last weekend of next month."

Michael hoped that Dr. Sparks, their botanist friend, had made some new discoveries about the plants she was growing from seeds they'd given her. They had gotten to be good friends with the Sparks family at an RV campground on their Florida vacation.

Michael said, "But we can't leave the plants home alone a whole weekend."

Norman told Mom, "It's your turn to stay home with them. Dad did it last time we went to the Sparkses."

"That won't be necessary," she replied. "The plants are invited, too."

"Oh, no," said Dad. "I don't want to travel with those plants again. The Florida trip was enough. And it's a five-hour drive from here to the

Sparkses. Call her back and tell her we can't come."

Mom said, "But this is for a really big event. The Natural History Museum there is opening a display of lifelike mechanical dinosaurs that weekend. And they're showing live plants that also lived in dinosaur times. Since ours are relatives of newly discovered fossil plants, they're doing a special display on them. Susan's lending the museum little ones that she grew from the seeds we gave her. But our big ones are more spectacular, so Susan said the museum would like to have them."

Norman protested, "I can't leave Fluffy in a museum. He'd miss me. And he and Stanley might get in trouble."

"Don't worry," said Mom. "They'll only be there for the opening weekend. And you and Michael get to spend Saturday night in the museum at a special sleep-over event for kids. Max and Sarah Sparks will go, too."

"Sleep in a museum?" exclaimed Norman. "With those dinosaur skeletons we saw there before? That'll be really scary!" He looked delighted.

"That'll be great," said Michael.

Mom said, "We drive to the Sparkses' Friday night and take the plants into the museum Saturday morning. The boys spend the night with them at the sleep-over. If Stanley and Fluffy start doing anything weird, the boys'll be right

5

there to stop them. Then we come home Sunday night."

"I don't know," said Dad. "It's such a big hassle to lug those plants anywhere. We'd have to rent an RV again. Or a truck."

Mom added, "Susan said the museum will pay our travel costs. And she invited us to stay at their house. The trip won't cost us anything."

"Hmm," said Dad, starting to look interested.

"And Susan's going to get someone at the museum to give us a behind-the-scenes tour—all the parts that visitors don't usually get to see. And she also said that we could visit a dig the museum is running."

"What are they digging up?" asked Dad.

"I don't know," she replied. "Probably fossils. Any ancient stuff they can find, I suppose."

"Dinosaurs?" asked Michael.

"I don't think any dinosaurs have been found around that part of the country," said Mom. "But then all I know about digs is what I've seen on TV or read in *National Geographic*."

Dad said, "Visiting a dig would be fascinating. When I was little, I had a secret desire to be an archeologist and dig up ancient stuff. OK, let's go. It'll be educational for the boys."

Michael was thrilled. A trip like this would be worth all the extra work of taking the plants along. Norman was so excited that he ran over to his best friend Bob's house to tell him the news.

A few minutes later, their neighbor, Mrs. Smith, rapped on the kitchen window. Mom opened the back door and invited her in. As Mom poured her some coffee, Mrs. Smith said, "I hear you're going to visit your botany friend and sleep in a museum."

Dad laughed. "Either you have ESP or you ran into Norman on your way over here."

Michael said, "Norman has the fastest mouth in town."

"He was really excited about sleeping in a museum," Mrs. Smith said. She asked Dad, "Why on earth do you want to sleep in a museum?"

"Just the boys will do that," he said. "It's a kid thing."

Mrs. Smith said, "I'll be glad to keep an eye on the house while you're away. And water the plants."

Mom explained why they were taking the plants along. "But we'd be glad to have you keep an eye on the house," said Dad.

Mrs. Smith was smiling broadly. Michael wondered why she was so happy about their trip.

"The reason I came over," she said, "is to tell you good news. My son's getting married!"

"Shawn? That's wonderful!" exclaimed Mom. "Who is he marrying?"

"Her name is Belinda. They met in college, so they've known each other quite a while. She teaches fourth grade in Elmville, where he works.

I really like her. She's a wonderful person. You're all invited to the wedding, so be sure to save the date." She pointed to the day on the wall calendar. Mom wrote on it, "Shawn's wedding."

"That's the weekend after our trip to the Sparkses'," she said.

Dad asked, "Are they getting married in Elmville?"

"No, at our church here. They asked me to help arrange everything."

"That's a lot of work," commented Mom.

"Yes, but I love to plan things," Mrs. Smith said.

"You did a great job on the neighborhood Fourth of July party," said Mom.

"Yeah," said Dad, chuckling. "That was a day none of us will ever forget."

"We did have a good time, didn't we," said Mrs. Smith. "People are still talking about the parade. And about how Norman served the mustard at the picnic—squirting it with his Super Splasher Water Blaster."

Michael muttered, "How could anybody forget."

"That Norman!" exclaimed Mrs. Smith. "He's so cute!"

Mom said, "If there's anything we can do to help, just let us know."

"I may take you up on that," said Mrs. Smith.

Michael scraped up the last few Bunch-O-Crunch flakes sticking to the sides of his bowl.

He had been to a few weddings and thought they were boring. The food had been great, though. He hoped he didn't have to get dressed up. But Shawn was a friend of his, so he wouldn't mind going to this wedding. Besides, if it turned out to be anything like Mrs. Smith's Fourth of July plans, it could be another day they would never forget.

Chapter 2

At school Michael told Chad Palmer, Brad Chan, and Jason Greensmith the news about the trip. Pat Jenkins overheard them talking and told a few dozen others. By the end of morning recess, the news was spreading fast. Norman also told lots of kids in his side of the building where the lower grades were.

Down the lunchroom lines and from table to table the story was repeated, getting bigger as it went. By the end of the day, Michael had heard several versions. His family was moving away to live in an art museum. They were going to Canada to dig up a tyrannosaurus rex. A live dinosaur had been captured in Ohio and was secretly locked up in the Cleveland Zoo's rainforest building.

The principal, Mr. Leedy, told Michael how lucky he and his family were to be going on an expedition to Mongolia to hunt for dinosaur eggs. Michael explained how it was only a weekend trip to a museum with a one-day stop at a dig.

"Oh," said Mr. Leedy, looking a bit disappointed. "I'm sure that will be interesting, too."

By the next morning, some first-graders had convinced themselves that a live tyrannosaurus was rampaging through Cleveland, knocking buildings down. When Mr. Leedy heard that, he announced the true story on the PA to set everybody straight.

For the trip, Dad arranged to rent a smaller RV than the one they had driven to Florida. They wouldn't be living in it this time, so they didn't need such a big one.

Mom bought an answering machine because her mother kept telling her they ought to have one. Grandma got irritated when she called them and nobody was home. She was a busy person and wanted to be able to leave a message.

Norman was delighted with the new machine. He kept going over to Bob's and calling home to leave messages. Then he and Bob would race home and listen to themselves on the playback. If Mom, Dad, or Michael answered before he could leave a message, Norman would squawk, "Hang up! Hang up!" So Mom had a talk with Bob's mother. That was the end of the silly messages from Bob's house.

*   *   *

One evening, Mom had to call Michael to the dinner table twice. That was unusual. She looked into the boys' room and found him reading *Smithsonian* magazine. Grandma had given the family a subscription, but Michael always grabbed it first.

"Come eat," she said. "Right now!"

When he got to the table, she asked, "What's in that magazine that interests you more than dinner?"

"Pitcher plants," he replied. "They're amazing."

Norman looked surprised. "They play baseball?" he asked.

"No, not that kind of pitcher. More like the kind you pour with. Only these don't pour. There's a pool of liquid inside. Bugs crawl in or fall in and get digested. They're meat-eating plants."

"Yuck," commented Norman.

Just to bother his brother, Michael added, "Yummy, munchy, crunchy, squishy, squashy, delicious bugs!"

Norman scrunched up his face and made a gagging noise.

Dad said, "Stop it, you two. No gross-outs at the table."

"He started it," said Norman.

"And I'm stopping it," said Dad. "Let's change the subject. Any suggestions about what we should do about a greenhouse?"

"I don't know," said Mom. "What do you think?"

Dad replied, "We can go broke slowly from buying socks, or we can go broke fast from buying a greenhouse."

Michael suggested, "The Sparkses have a greenhouse. Maybe when we go there we can ask them where to buy a cheap one."

At bedtime, the boys went through their usual routine. They put Stanley and Fluffy's favorite flavors of socks on the floor—white with brown stripes, which they called fudge ripple, and a couple of strawberry pink ones. They smeared some orange juice on the rolled-up leaves to prevent the plants from going to the kitchen and helping themselves to juice from the refrigerator. This had caused a major sticky mess in the past.

When the boys were settled in bed, Norman said, "We could teach Fluffy and Stanley to play baseball. Then they'd be pitcher plants."

Michael replied, "Fluffy can be a pitcher plant, and Stanley can be a catcher plant. Then we can get them jobs playing for the White Sox. Or the Red Sox."

They both laughed so loud that Mom came in to see what was so funny. When they told her, she started to laugh, too.

"If you can get Fluffy and Stanley a job with the White Sox or Red Sox," she said, "maybe I can get my panty hose a job there, too, because they're always getting runs."

As Michael was drifting off to sleep, he thought that it was probably impossible to pitch a ball with a vine, but maybe Stanley could catch one with Michael's baseball glove. The next morning, he started trying to get Stanley to hold the glove.

Sunday morning Michael as usual hoped to sleep late, but he woke up because there was no noise. Norman and Fluffy weren't there. The door was open. From the living room down the hall he could hear Norman singing, "Put your right vine in, no, your right vine, this one . . ."

Michael was surprised to see that Stanley was gone, too. When he went into the hall, he saw his plant pulling himself along to the living room on his skateboard. Michael followed.

Norman was moving one of Fluffy's vines to show the plant what to do. Michael sprawled on the couch to watch.

"How's it going?" he asked.

"Not too good," replied Norman. "Fluffy still doesn't get the part about right vine, left vine. He puts any old vine in."

Michael suggested, "Maybe it's because he has more than one of each. If I had four right hands, I wouldn't know which one to put in either."

Norman sang, "Put all your right vines in." Fluffy put forward vines from all over himself—right, left, and the middle.

Norman decided to change the words to go with

what Fluffy was already doing. He sang, "Put any old vines in, and shake them all about." Whirling vines and leaves seemed to fill the room as Fluffy danced joyfully in all directions. Stanley joined in. Then they stopped.

"Wow," said Norman. "I guess that's the only part they really like to do. I didn't expect Fluffy to do that until we got to the 'Put your whole self in' part."

"He put his whole self in all right," said Michael. By waving all his vines at once, Fluffy had gotten totally tangled up. Norman unwound the vines carefully.

Then he got his Super Splasher Water Blaster to give Fluffy his morning watering. Michael had fallen asleep on the couch, so Norman watered Stanley, too.

Since the Hokey Pokey wasn't going well, he wondered what he might teach his plant next. Fluffy could already roll a ball back when Norman rolled it to him. The kitchen chores the boys had taught them had unfortunately ended in a gigantic mess. But both plants did some dusting around the house, mostly to help keep the boys' room clean. And they could run themselves around by holding on to the boys' remote control trucks with one vine and operating the controls with another. But Mom had locked up the trucks when she found out about that.

Norman thought the plants must be tired from

Hokey Pokeying, especially Fluffy. So he decided to do something that he and his plant really enjoyed—listening to himself sing. Norman loved to sing, even though he sounded terrible. Two of his favorite songs were "Oh, Susanna" and "Camptown Races," especially the "doo-dah" parts. To hear Norman howling "oh, do-dah-day" at the top of his lungs was truly an ear-splitting experience.

At Norman's first big high note, Michael awoke with a jolt, like a cartoon character zapped by lightning. Taking Stanley along, he went back to bed.

As the family prepared for their trip, Mrs. Smith kept them posted about the wedding plans.

"Shawn and Belinda want to do this for as little money as possible," she said.

Mom asked, "Have you decided what you'd like us to do to help?"

"Would you be able to bake about twelve dozen of those delicious rolls you make? So many friends have offered to help that I've asked some people to fix food for the reception."

"I'd be glad to," said Mom. "Anything else?"

"One thing the boys could do is fill the bags of birdseed to throw after the wedding."

"There's going to be birds at the wedding?" asked Norman.

"No," said Mrs. Smith. "People used to throw rice at the bride and groom when they came out of the church. But that made a mess all over the sidewalk. When you throw birdseed instead, birds come and eat it all. No mess."

"Neat," said Norman.

She said, "I'll give you boys a couple of hundred little bags that will each hold a handful. Then you tie them shut with satin ribbons. Michael, would you pass out the bags to the guests outside the church?"

Michael wasn't thrilled about having to tie a lot of little bags up with ribbons, but he said OK.

"One other thing," said Mrs. Smith. "At the Fourth of July picnic, everybody got a big kick out of Norman squeezing mustard on their sandwiches with his Water Blaster. It was so cute! So I want him to use it for the chocolate syrup at the wedding reception. We're having frozen yogurt with the cake. Belinda likes that better than ice cream."

Norman's eyes lit up.

"Oh," said Mom. "That's not such a good idea. Every time he's put something gooey in that thing, we've had a Blaster disaster—maple syrup all over a TV reporter, grape jelly on our friend Susan Sparks, and mustard all over Norman. Not to mention the night he sprayed almost enough water all over the boys' room to scuba dive in. He'd better leave his Blaster home that day. You might wind up with chocolate syrup all over the bride. Not just the frozen yogurt."

Norman protested, "But I'll be really, really careful! I'll tell her to stand back!"

Mom replied, "Running around the reception with that thing loaded with chocolate syrup would be asking for trouble. Things could go wrong just getting it there in the car!"

Mrs. Smith suggested, "He can bring his Blaster empty. I'll order huge cans of syrup, and we'll fill up the Blaster in the church kitchen just before we serve the dessert. That way, there won't be any chance of chocolate in the wrong places."

"Well," said Mom, trying to think of another excuse.

Mrs. Smith put an arm around Norman, who was standing next to her chair. "I'm sure he'll be very, very careful," she said. "Won't you?"

Norman nodded. "Very, very," he assured Mom.

Mrs. Smith asked Dad if he would help set up tables for the reception in the church meeting hall. He said yes.

After Mrs. Smith left, Dad asked Mom, "How did we get so involved in this wedding? Are you sure you want to do all this stuff?"

Mom explained, "She's a wonderful neighbor. She looks out for all the kids on the street. And she's always been especially nice to Norman. When he was lost, she was the first one out searching. And Shawn has been a good friend to Michael. He even turned some of his lawn mowing customers over to him when he moved away.

Helping them with this wedding is the least we can do."

That evening Mom went shopping by herself to buy a wedding present for Shawn and Belinda.

When she got back, Norman asked, "Where's the present?"

"I had it sent to them," she said. "Some plates in their china pattern."

"Then what's in the packages?" asked Dad.

From one Mom pulled a beautiful green dress. "I needed a new outfit. The wedding is a good reason to buy one," she said.

"It looks great," said Dad. "How much did it cost?"

"Never mind," she said. "I'm paying for it with money I earned myself."

From another bag she pulled a pair of green high-heeled shoes.

"Very glamorous," said Dad. "You don't wear high heels very often."

"They're perfect with the dress. None of my old shoes would look right with it."

Norman said, "Didn't you buy me anything?"

"Yes," replied Mom. "I got you and Michael some plant food." She handed him a large bag of socks from the Save-A-Lot discount store.

Norman asked, "Do we have to get dressed up for the wedding, too?"

"Yes," said Mom. "Long-sleeved shirt, tie, good pants, good shoes, good socks. No fudge ripple."

19

"Why not?" whined Norman.

"Because to go with your good navy blue pants, you'll have to wear blueberry."

To take his mind off the bad news that he would have to wear a tie for the wedding, Michael looked around for something to read. He picked up a gardening supply catalog and took it to the kitchen. He peeled a banana and sat at the table, eating and looking at pictures of greenhouses.

Norman came in and said, "What are you doing?"

"Nothing," answered Michael, who wanted to be alone without Norman pestering him. Norman got a banana and sat down. He started humming. Michael ignored him and kept on leafing through the catalog.

One strange ad offered "Insects by mail." He read it and said out loud, "Amazing!"

"What? What is it?" asked Norman, coming over to look.

Michael said, "You can order bugs by mail for greenhouses or gardens."

"Why?" asked Norman.

Michael explained, "If bad bugs attack your plants, you can send away for good kinds of bugs—ones that are their natural enemies—to eat them up. That way you don't have to use poisonous chemicals to kill them."

Norman said, "Like a battle of the bugs?"

Michael replied, "More like a picnic of the bugs."

"Ugh," remarked Norman. "But how can anybody mail bugs? Does the mailman bring them with the letters and magazines? What if the bugs got loose in the post office? They could crawl in people's letters and surprise them when they open the envelopes!"

Michael said, "They must be sent in escape-proof boxes."

But Norman continued, "If they got out in the post office, the post office would have to send away for another kind of bugs to eat the ones running around there. Then they'd have to send away for another kind to eat the new bugs that ate the old bugs. They'd have to keep getting more and more bugs, and every new bunch would get bigger and fatter. Bugs could take over the post office!"

Michael got a mental picture of a tall, fat bug selling stamps and weighing packages. "I don't think so," he said.

Dad came in to get a banana. He asked, "What are you guys doing?"

"Just eating bananas," said Norman.

Chapter 3

Norman kept complaining about not being allowed to play with the answering machine any more. To show him that it wasn't a toy, Dad said he would let Norman re-record the answering message in a serious voice. Then Norman could go to Bob's, call home, and listen to himself answer the phone.

Dad coached him on what to say: "You have reached 555–4321. When the beep sounds, please leave a message, and we'll call you back as soon as we can. Thank you."

Norman got it right on the third try. As Dad operated the machine to record, Norman watched closely to see how he did it.

At school Jason leaned over to Michael's desk and said, "When you go to that dig, bring home some dino bones. We could make a lot of money selling those to other kids."

Michael replied, "I don't think there are going to be any dino bones there. Even if there were, you're not supposed to take them."

"Then maybe you could just put a couple of little ones in your pocket. One for you and one for me."

"No," said Michael.

"Or some other fossils," said Jason. "I'm sure that museum has plenty already."

"Forget it," said Michael.

"I gave you my plant," said Jason.

"Gave?" said Michael. "You grew that plant from a seed you took from me. And Norman and I helped you out by taking it away before your mother found out you were growing it behind your garage. It was attacking anybody who came near. You couldn't handle it. The way you treated it turned it into Stanley's evil twin. You're lucky that Norman tamed it down and we took it away."

Jason said, "You made money off it, though."

"It was lucky we could sell it to a botanical garden. It's a place that takes good care of plants."

"Is it acting up there?" asked Jason.

"I don't think so. We probably would have heard if it was." Michael hoped they would never hear about that plant again.

The night before the trip, the family packed up to be ready to leave right after school the next day.

When the boys got home Friday afternoon, the RV waited in the driveway. They helped Dad hoist Fluffy and Stanley up the narrow RV steps. They guided their tops through the open air vents in the roof. Michael climbed up the ladder on the back of the RV to put heavy plastic sheeting over the tops of plants. He tucked the edges in. Dad secured the plastic inside with wide tape.

"That will keep them warm enough and protect them from the wind," said Dad.

Bob and Mrs. Smith waved good-bye, and they drove off on their weekend adventure.

On the way, Mom made the boys do their homework. Later, she fixed dinner in the RV's tiny kitchen. They ate watching scenery whiz by. Then Mom took a turn driving so Dad could eat and relax a while.

They arrived at the Sparkses' house about 8 P.M. Dr. Sparks, her husband, and their two children came out and piled into the RV to greet them.

Max, a year younger than Norman, and Sarah, who was Michael's age, were as interested in seeing Stanley and Fluffy again as their mother, the botanist, was. The boys told the Sparkses about their plants' latest activities.

Michael inquired, "How are the six plants in your greenhouse doing?"

"We don't have them anymore," replied Sarah. "My mom made us put them in the research center with the other ones."

Max said, "We go visit them there. They're learning to do different things."

"Like what?" asked Norman.

"Pick up trash and throw it in a trash can," said Max. "They're getting pretty good at it."

Dr. Sparks reminded them, "We turn lights on them at night and keep them dark during the day, so they eat and move in the daytime as if it were night. That way it's easier for us to study them. And we don't have to pay people extra to work nights."

Sarah said, "We visit them there some Saturdays."

Max told Norman, "I still sing to mine when I visit."

"Did you try the Hokey Pokey?" asked Norman. They went out of the RV with their heads together in conversation.

Michael asked Sarah, "Why did you have to put your plants in the research center?"

"My mom and dad found out Max was setting his alarm clock and getting up in the middle of the night to see them eat socks. One day he fell asleep in school. His teacher called because she was worried about him. And he fell asleep at the dinner table. He went face down in his mashed potatoes."

Michael asked, "Why didn't they just take away his alarm clock?"

"Some windowpanes in our greenhouse got broken. My mom thought the plants did it when they were playing. She said the research center could take better care of them."

"Do you miss them?"

"No, she got us some great new plants."

"What kind?"

"Come on. I'll show you." She led the way to the small greenhouse behind their home.

Max and Norman were already there. The greenhouse was dark. Through the glass roof, Michael could see the night sky.

With a flashlight, Max was showing off his new plant, a Venus flytrap about six inches high. Its three oval green two-part leaves, fringed with slender spikes, stood open at an angle.

"Don't you have any lights in here?" asked Michael.

"Yes," she said, "but we can't turn them on."

"Can we see it eat a bug?" asked Norman before Michael could ask her why.

"Hardly any bugs ever come by," replied Max. "But when one does, bam! The trap shuts on it!"

Norman said, "I saw one of these do that in a video in school. But I never saw one do it in person. Let's go find a bug!" They started crawling around the floor.

Stepping over them, Michael said, "I hope your mother didn't find this Venus flytrap growing in the wild. Anybody who swipes one of these from the wild in North Carolina has to pay a two thousand dollar fine. For pitcher plants, too."

"How do you know that?" asked Sarah.

"*Smithsonian* magazine," he answered casually. "They had a good article about meat-eating plants." Sarah looked impressed. "And one about strangler vines," he added. "They're real monsters. We have a subscription," he boasted. "But you could get it at a library."

Sarah said, "The research center grew hundreds of these flytraps from plant cells in a special growing liquid in a flask. That's a laboratory bottle," she added.

"I know what a flask is," said Michael.

Max and Norman were having no luck at bug finding and gave up. Norman wanted to know, "Won't it starve to death if it doesn't get bugs to eat?"

"No," said Michael. "The *Smithsonian* article said they don't need bugs to live. But if they eat them, they grow better. Digesting bugs gives them nutrients that they don't get from the soil where they grow wild."

"Sort of like vitamin pills," said Sarah.

"Flying vitamins," said Norman, laughing. "Yuck!"

"Yuck!" agreed Max. They were interrupted by a tapping on the greenhouse glass. Three faces peered in.

"Who's that?" asked Norman.

Sarah replied, "Neighbors." She unlocked the outside door. A mother and two girls came in.

27

"Good," said the mother. "We're not too late."

Michael wondered for what.

Sarah told the woman, "It'll be pretty soon." Two more families arrived. The greenhouse was getting crowded. Mom and Dad squeezed in along with Dr. Sparks and her husband.

"I've always wanted to see one of these," said Mom.

Everyone seemed to know what they were going to see except Michael. While he had been acting like a know-it-all about bug eaters, Sarah had not let him in on this.

He turned to look at the plant everyone else was watching expectantly. Large, with dark green leaves, it had some closed-up, big white flower buds which were easy to see in the dark.

Suddenly, to Michael's astonishment, the plant began to tremble, as if it were nervous. Then one of the buds slowly began to open.

"What is this?" Michael asked Mom.

"It's a night-blooming cereus. I've heard about these, but I've never seen one. This is really a treat."

The bud continued slowly opening. Michael thought he couldn't see the petals moving, but every time he looked away for a few moments and looked back at it, it had opened more.

A neighbor said, "No matter how many times I see this, it's still a thrill."

Dr. Sparks told the others, "When the flower

is completely open, it'll be about twelve inches wide." She told Mom and Dad, "Every night people come to see this. We may have to start taking reservations. It's turning into a tourist attraction. If we're not home, they stand outside to watch. We're constantly cleaning fingerprints and nose prints off the glass panes."

The people all chatted as they watched the plant. It was like a little party. Mr. Sparks and Dad discussed greenhouses.

The flower's sweet smell filled the greenhouse.

"Where did you get this?" Michael asked Sarah.

"My mom got it for me from somebody who was moving to Alaska and couldn't take it along. She wanted to find a good home for it. It's a very old plant that was passed down from her grandmother. I promised to take good care of it."

"Lucky you," remarked Michael.

"Yes," she agreed with a big grin. "Did you know that the flowers of night-blooming plants are white so they attract the night moths that pollinate them? White flowers can be seen in the dark."

"Maybe night-blooming plants are related to Stanley and Fluffy. They're night-eating," said Michael.

"In Hawaii," said Sarah, "there's a famous wall that's covered with night-blooming cereus plants. They also grow along some roads there."

"I'd like to see that," said Norman.

Sarah said, "We're going to Hawaii next year on our vacation. It's a great place to go if you're interested in botany. And my mother and I want to take hula lessons."

Max said, "My dad and I are going fishing there."

Michael looked at the cereus. The flower was still unfolding. In the dark, its many long, slender petals looked like a burst of white fireworks standing still.

After a couple of hours it was time for the kids to go to bed. Sarah was planning to stay up late with her plant. "I took a nap after school," she said. "When this flower is completely open, it'll be as big as a dinner plate. I don't want to miss that."

Michael tried to persuade Mom and Dad to let him stay up with her. But he kept yawning when he was telling them he wasn't tired, so they made him go back into the house with Norman and Max.

Chapter 4

Dad and Mr. Sparks brought Stanley and Fluffy into the house for the night and parked them in the living room.

Dr. Sparks told Mom and Dad, "We've got the guest bedroom ready for you. The boys will all sleep up in Max's room."

Norman asked, "Where are our plants going to sleep?"

"Downstairs here in the living room," she replied.

"But Fluffy and Stanley are used to being in our room at night. If they're not with us, they might start wandering around to try to find us," he warned. "They might knock things over."

"Then we'll have to carry them up to Max's room," she decided.

"But," protested Norman, "they might accidentally get out of the room. They could fall down the stairs in the middle of the night and get killed. They're not used to stairs. We don't have any at our house."

Dad said, "Lugging them upstairs *is* too much trouble."

Mr. Sparks said, "And we'd just have to lug them down again in the morning. Let's have the boys sleep in the living room. Then everybody will be happy—plants and humans." The boys went to get their sleeping bags.

Long after everyone had gone to sleep, Dr. Sparks, who had set her alarm clock, came downstairs and sent Sarah up to bed. Then she curled up on the living room couch with a blanket and a notebook. She watched with fascination as Stanley and Fluffy sucked up their socks, schlurped and burped. Stanley picked up a T-shirt Max had dropped and dusted the furniture with it. Since Dr. Sparks was sitting still, he also dusted her. Fluffy patted Norman's head with a vine, and tugged his sleeping bag flap up snugly under his chin.

After the plants settled down, Dr. Sparks fell asleep, too, nestled in her blanket on the couch. Early in the morning, an irritating noise woke her up. She stepped over Michael and two empty sleeping bags to follow the sound. In the kitchen, she found Norman showing Max how Fluffy could drive himself around with Max's remote control racing car.

After breakfast, Dad and the boys loaded Stanley and Fluffy into the RV. Dr. Sparks noticed that Max was sniffing and felt his forehead.

"No fever," she said, "but if you're getting a cold, you'd better stay home tonight."

They all rode to the museum in the RV.

"Pull up by the front entrance," said Dr. Sparks. "They usually bring exhibits in by the loading dock in back. Since these plants roll easily, I told them we wouldn't need to do that."

The museum wasn't open yet, but a dark-haired man in jeans was waiting for them. He bounded into the RV to see the plants.

Dr. Sparks said, "This is Joe Maxwell. He's the paleobotanist here."

"What kind of botanist is that?" asked Norman.

"I'm an ancient plant scientist," Joe Maxwell explained. "I mean, I'm not ancient. The plants I work with are. Paleo means ancient or prehistoric. Botany is the science of plants. So paleobotany means the science of ancient plants."

When Michael called him Dr. Maxwell, he said, "Call me Joe." He looked closely at Stanley and Fluffy.

"Magnificent!" he exclaimed. "The discovery of those previously unknown fossil plants in Asia was thrilling, but finding that you and Susan had live ones—that was beyond my wildest dreams! Of course, these are smaller than the fossil ones."

"But ours are the biggest ones," said Norman.

Joe replied, "They are now, but some of today's plants whose relatives lived in dinosaur times grew much bigger then. Like club mosses. They get about this big now." He held his hand about four feet above the floor. "But fossils show that they used to get as high as thirty feet tall or more."

Norman and Max looked puzzled, as if they couldn't picture that.

Joe explained, "I'm six feet tall. Now picture another six-foot-tall person standing on my head, and another one standing on his head. And another one. And one more. That's what thirty feet tall looks like—five six-foot people standing on each other's heads."

Max and Norman giggled.

Michael asked, "How big do you think our kind of plants used to get?"

"I don't know. The fossils may be from forty-foot plants. But that's just a guess. There's a lot of research still to be done. Seeing how big yours and Susan's get eventually will give us some clues."

Mom remarked, "These better not get to be forty feet tall!"

They rolled Stanley and Fluffy into the museum, through the large lobby, and on into the huge dinosaur hall. Towering above them were the two dinosaur skeletons the boys had seen on their last visit.

Now spaced around those stood whole dinosaurs with bumpy skins of many colors. A twelve-foot-high tyrannosaurus, blue-gray with a red throat, leaned forward on its massive hind legs. A gray triceratops with sharp horns stood squarely on all fours. At the feet of a pair of light brown, duck-billed hadrosaurs lay a nest of large eggs.

There were more dinosaurs, but Michael's attention was drawn to the less spectacular attractions—small trees growing in large containers. Their signs said they were living relatives of prehistoric trees—gingkos, magnolias, cycads, and a monkey puzzle tree from the Andes Mountains in South America. A pine tree that would have made a good little Christmas tree had light green needles. Michael looked at the sign. It was a dawn redwood. These had been thought extinct for millions of years until three were found in China in the 1940s. Dr. Sparks had told him about it a few months ago.

Norman and Max were running around awestruck, looking at the dinosaurs.

Michael and Sarah looked awestruck at the dawn redwood.

"This is wonderful!" he said, forgetting to act cool.

35

"It is," agreed Sarah. "Did you know it loses its needles in the winter time?"

Michael tried not to look surprised. He said, "Then it would make a weird-looking Christmas tree." Sarah smiled.

Mom said, "I thought dinosaurs were green."

Joe explained, "Nobody's sure what color they were or what noises they made. The people who built these based their guesses on the latest research."

Norman said, "They're not doing anything. Aren't they supposed to move?"

Joe said, "They won't be turned on until just before the museum opens at ten. Come on, let's go to Gallery Six. That's where your plants will be on exhibit."

"Electric dinosaurs!" said Norman. "Cool!"

Dad muttered to Mr. Sparks, "I'd hate to have to pay the electricity bill for this."

"Me, too," agreed Mr. Sparks.

On they went through more large rooms with more dinosaurs and plants.

"Here we are," said Joe, leading them into Gallery Six. A green stegosaurus took up a lot of space. Sticking up along the ridge of its back were two rows of pointed plates. Four spikes stuck up from its tail. The short front legs and huge back ones had claws on the feet.

Joe showed the boys where to put Stanley and Fluffy on opposite sides of the dinosaur. Nearby on the wall was a display about the plant fossil discovery, with big slabs of dark rock. The shapes of thick stems, leaves, and vines pressed into the rocks looked as if they had come from a very big brother of Stanley and Fluffy. The impressions were so clear the boys could see the veins in the leaves. A sign explained about the fossils and the living plants that matched them.

"These aren't the real fossils," Joe said. "Those are in Asia. Even if we had them, they'd be too valuable to put out. These are exact copies."

He got Dad and Mr. Sparks to help him drag a heavy railing mounted on posts across in front of the plants and dinosaur. "This will keep visitors from getting close enough to touch," he explained.

Along the same side of the gallery was an area with walls almost all around it, like a smaller room built inside the bigger one. On one wall was a big sign:

SEE THE PLANTS MOVE—BETWEEN 11 A.M. AND 2 P.M.

Dr. Sparks led them all into the space enclosed by these walls, which didn't go all the way to the ceiling. Up on a platform stood six junior versions of Stanley and Fluffy, Dr. Sparks's plants from the research center. They ranged in size from two feet to three feet tall. The walls blocked out most of the bright light that shone on the rest of the gallery.

"I get it," said Norman. "This is so they'll think it's nighttime now."

"Correct," said Dr. Sparks. She patted the leaves of one plant. "These are ones we've trained to pick up litter. Then they get cut up bits of socks as a reward."

"Like doggie treats," said Sarah.

"I want to see that," said Mom.

"Even though it's only a possibility for the far-off future," continued Dr. Sparks, "I'll still think someday there could be millions of these plants picking up litter all over the world."

Norman said huffily, "Plants shouldn't have to do that! People should clean up their own messes!"

"Unfortunately," said Dr. Sparks, "not everyone is as neat as you, Norman. When you grow up, you should get a job cleaning up the environment. You'd be excellent at that."

Joe laughed. "You could start with my office," he told Norman. "People tell me there's so much stuff on my desk you could do an archeological dig there."

A museum guard came in. "We're opening in five minutes," he said. He went behind the stegosaurus and turned on a hidden switch. For a moment, nothing happened. Then the huge creature slowly raised its scaly green head and turned it toward Max and Norman. It rolled its eyes to look right at them, opened its mouth, and quietly snorted.

The noise startled Stanley and Fluffy. They quivered a little, but settled down right away.

"This is great!" exclaimed Norman.

"Really great!" said Max.

The dinosaur closed its mouth, turned its head back, and stopped moving.

"What else is it going to do?" Norman asked the guard.

"That was it," he answered. "It does the same thing over and over."

Dr. Sparks said she would stay with the plants while Joe took the rest of them on a museum tour. First they went to see the other dinosaurs move.

One duck-billed hadrosaur turned the top of its body as if it heard something dangerous sneaking up. The other bobbed above the nest, where their babies popped out of the eggs and back in again.

The tyrannosaurus raised its huge head, showed its big sharp teeth, and roared.

Dad remarked, "I wouldn't want to get within chomping distance of that one."

"Me neither," agreed Max.

Then Joe led them to the parts of the museum where the public was not allowed. They came to a door with a NO ADMITTANCE sign.

Joe patted his pockets. "I forgot my keys

again," he said. He went to get a guard, who unlocked the door and followed them inside and down a hall.

They stopped at a door marked PALEOBOTANY. The guard unlocked it. He asked Joe, "You sure you know where your keys are?"

Joe replied, "They must be on my desk. Thanks, Charlie."

"If you don't find them," said Charlie, "call the guard desk, and I'll come let you out."

Dad asked, "You can't let yourself out?"

Joe explained, "We need a key to get in and another one to get out. That's not unusual in museums where valuable collections are stored."

He pushed the door all the way open for them to enter. Michael was surprised. He had expected a laboratory. But this was a large room like a basement, with gray cinder block walls and no windows. Many rows of storage units with wide shallow drawers had narrow aisles between them. On large tables sat slabs of rock with plant shapes in them. In a corner stood a big chunk of a tree trunk that had turned to stone.

Michael peeked through an open door into an office. A computer sat on a small table surrounded by boxes full of papers. Thin magazines with no pictures on their covers were stacked all over. Sagging shelves were stuffed with books. An old couch was piled with more junk, leaving no room to sit.

Joe began searching through a gigantic mess on his desk—heaps of papers, books, rocks, letters, pictures, crumpled sandwich wrappers, and a wrinkled Happy Birthday balloon that had lost most of its air.

Michael felt right at home in this room. It reminded him of the way his half of his and Norman's room used to look—before Mom and Dad had told him he had to keep it clean if he wanted to keep Stanley.

Norman came in jingling a bunch of keys. "These were by some rocks on a table," he said. Joe thanked him and put the keys in his pocket.

Norman looked around at the mess. "What happened?" he asked. "Vandalism?"

Joe smiled. "No, it's this way on purpose. When my stuff is all spread out, I know exactly where everything is."

A phone started ringing, but there was no phone in sight. Joe moved some papers to uncover it. After he hung up, another stack toppled over on it.

Joe led them into another large room. "This is where we prepare the fossils—clean and preserve them. Sometimes we have to chip rock away to free them, or use acid to dissolve the rock."

Big laundry sinks had splatters of dried mud caked around the edges. Tools and pairs of safety glasses were strewn atop big tables. Cardboard boxes full of rocks wrapped in old newspapers stood around on the floor.

41

The boys looked closely at a huge rock with a jumble of small bones sticking out of it.

"Small dinosaurs," explained Joe. "One of our expert volunteers is working on chipping the rock away to get them out. He's been at it for months. It's slow, delicate work. We also match up things that are found broken or scattered or crushed. That takes a lot of patience, too."

Joe showed them where the dinosaur and other prehistoric animal bones were stored. He even let them hold a few.

They moved on to see the anthropology department. There students were arranging bones on a big table.

Norman asked, "What kind of bones are those?"

"Human," said Joe.

Mom said, "This is creepy."

They took an elevator to the basement, where Joe unlocked another NO ADMITTANCE door. On they went through departments that had vast collections of dead birds, mammals, bugs, reptiles, fish, and plants. They met some scientists who were at work even though it was Saturday.

Michael asked, "Why do they have so much stuff put away here?"

"We collect all these specimens to study and compare them," replied Joe. "This is one of the ways we learn about nature."

From the next door Joe opened came a rush of very cold air. He turned on the lights. Surrounding them were huge animals. A ten-foot-tall brown grizzly bear was standing up with its front paws outstretched and teeth bared. A zebra and a water buffalo with curved horns stood next to three lions. On a long shelf lay an enormous alligator. Another shelf was filled with birds. Fortunately, none of them was moving.

"Are they statues?" asked Norman. "They look real."

"The skins are real," said Joe. "They're taxidermied. That means stuffed. This special cold room keeps them in good condition. The cold kills any insects that might get into them when they're out on display in warmer rooms."

Michael had never been nose to nose with a lion or a zebra before, so he took a good look.

On the way back to Gallery Six, Dad asked Joe about the dig they were going to visit.

"It's a place the land owners recently gave us permission to go on," he answered, "so we're just starting to search there. A good bunch of volunteers helps on weekends. I'll draw you a map so you can meet us there tomorrow morning. Have you ever been on a field trip like this before?"

"No," said Dad. "We're really looking forward to it. It's nice of you to let the kids come along."

Joe replied, "Oh, kids are good at finding fossils. Maybe because they're closer to the ground. Sometimes they see things that grownups miss.

And they like to pound rocks with hammers. I take my kids along whenever I can." He looked at his watch. "We'd better hurry," he said. "It's almost time for Susan's plants to show off."

Chapter 5

A crowd had gathered in Gallery Six. While they waited for the small plants to do something, they looked at Stanley and Fluffy and the fossil copies and watched the stegosaurus move.

Dr. Sparks was answering questions. She explained that dinosaurs like the stegosaurus lived by eating enormous quantities of plants.

A little girl at the front of the crowd inquired in a squeaky voice, "Is it gonna eat those plants?"

"No," her older sister informed her. "It's a fake. It's not going to eat anything."

"I wanna see it eat those plants," said the squeaky child.

"Be quiet," said her sister, "or it might eat you."

Nothing more was heard from the little girl.

Suddenly the crowd cried out, "OOOOH!" One

of the little plants had waved a vine as if to say hello to them all. Small children waved back.

One of Dr. Sparks's student assistants put a crumpled ball of paper beside that plant. It did a lot more vine waving. After a while it picked up the paper and dropped it into a little plastic wastebasket. The assistant offered the plant a small piece of sock. It grabbed it and sucked it into a rolled-up leaf with a not-very-loud schlurp. That was followed in a few moments by a dainty burp.

The crowd cheered and applauded. Then the student offered the plant a banana peel, a gum wrapper, an empty snack-sized raisin box, and a squashed tissue. The plant poked around with vines and, one by one, grabbed these things and tossed them in the wastebasket.

After each toss, the plant was rewarded with a bit of sock. After each schlurp, the crowd waited quietly for the burp. The burps seemed to be the most popular part of the act.

Michael whispered to Sarah, "They do tricks like trained dogs."

"Yes," she said. "Aren't they wonderful?"

"How long do they keep going?" he asked.

"Until they've eaten about two socks. The shortest ones stop at a sock and a half."

After the first performing plant had enough to eat, it lost interest in picking up any more trash.

46

There was a long lull while the six small plants just stood there, doing nothing. Children got fidgety. Families moved on. More people crowded in to wait.

Another plant lifted three of its vines and stretched as if waking up. It poked around at the trash, and grabbed a banana peel. The plant that had been through performing suddenly tried to grab the peel away. The crowd was treated to a plant tug-of-war. Dr. Sparks had to break it up.

Children in the crowd kept saying they wanted one of those plants. Some parents got annoyed when they found out they couldn't buy them in the museum gift shop. To one father who complained, a guard explained that the shop wasn't selling life-size mechanical dinosaurs either.

Michael and Norman stayed with Stanley and Fluffy all day except for lunch, snacks, and restroom breaks, when Dr. Sparks had an assistant take over. They answered so many questions and were stared at by so many people that the boys were glad when the museum closed at five-thirty. Michael felt as if he and Norman had been on exhibit, too.

They went out to dinner with Mom and Dad and the Sparks family. Max's sniffles were worse, so his mother said he had to stay home that night. Sarah had decided to stay home with her cereus. She explained that she had already been to a museum sleep-over last year.

Mom and Dad took the boys back to the museum with their sleeping bags at seven o'clock. Kids were arriving in droves.

There were activities all over the museum. The kids made dinosaur models and plaster casts of trilobite molds. There were small and large fossils they could touch. They got to put their feet in stone dinosaur tracks. A computer program showed how scientists figure out from tracks how fast dinosaurs walked or ran.

Joe was there with his two sons. He introduced them to Michael and Norman. One of the guards came by and told Joe with a grin, "This sleep-over is for kids."

Joe replied, "I'm a volunteer chaperone, so I'll be here all night. I go on duty at 3 A.M. I took a nap this afternoon, and I'm going to try to get some sleep on the couch in my office before my shift. But if I can't sleep, I'll do a little work."

"OK," said the guard. "Call me if you lock yourself out of your office again."

In the gift shop, Norman bought pencils with dinosaur pictures on them. He also got a yellow eraser shaped like a tyrannosaurus and a pair of brown socks with green stegosauruses all over them. He wanted to buy a dinosaur tie to wear to Shawn's wedding, but he didn't have enough money.

Michael considered blowing most of his money on a plant fossil. It was a small pointed leaf outlined in a chunk of sandstone. But he decided to think about it overnight and come back the next day.

At eight o'clock, all the kids trooped into the auditorium. First they saw a short movie about how the mechanical dinosaurs were made. Michael was fascinated to see the electronic innards that made them move. Then a woman showed slides and told facts about different kinds of dinos. Joe showed slides of fossil plants and what the world looked liked in different dinosaur eras.

Then a guy with a guitar led them all in singing "Old MacDonald Had a Farm," only he changed the farm animals to dinosaurs. So they were singing, "And on this farm, he had a brontosaurus, with a munch-munch here, and a munch-munch there. Here a munch, there a munch, everywhere a munch-munch." When they got to the duck-billed hadrosaurus, they quack-quacked. That ended with everyone laughing and applauding.

"Now we're going to do a dino dance," announced the guitar player. "I need some people to help."

Norman bounced eagerly in his seat, hoping to be noticed. Michael slumped down, trying to be invisible. One of the seven children the leader pointed to was Norman. They ran up the steps to the stage.

"This dance," the man said, "is called the Stegosaurus Stomp." Everyone laughed.

"Steggys have pointy faces, so put your hands together pointing outward," he instructed. "Hold them up in front of your nose. Good! Now turn right, left, right, left again!" He played a catchy tune while they turned.

To do the plates on the stegosaurus's back, he showed them how to cross their wrists and flap their hands in opposite directions. Next he got them to stomp.

Then he lined them up to act out being a whole dinosaur—one to be the face and front legs, four with hands over heads to be the plates along the back, then Norman as the back legs. The seventh lay on the floor to be the tail with his arms sticking up to be the spikes.

"OK, now everybody," called the leader. "Stand up!" With groans and laughter, the whole crowd got up.

He sang, "One, two, three, four! Do the steggy nose, left, bomp, bomp, bomp, right, bomp, bomp, bomp. Flap your steggy plates, flap, flap, flappity, flap. Now do the steggy toes, left, stomp, stomp, stomp, right, stomp, stomp, stomp! One more time!" The auditorium thundered with stomping. He sang the big finish: "We're doin' the Steg-gy Stomp!" The kids all collapsed into their seats, laughing.

"Up, up, up!" shouted the leader. "We're going to end with one everybody knows! The Hokey

Pokey!" He started strumming and singing. All the kids put their right hands in.

Michael was glad Stanley and Fluffy were not nearby. He glanced back up the aisle to the auditorium doors. They stood open, but Gallery Six was so far away that the sound probably wouldn't carry there.

Far off in Gallery Six, the music could be heard very faintly. Anyone listening there wouldn't have been able to make out the words. Fluffy and Stanley began swaying to the melody. Fluffy held out some vines, pulled them back, and held them out a little further. They bumped into the dinosaur, which had been turned off. Startled, Fluffy felt around the creature's side, as if trying to figure out what it was. Then he lost interest and went back to swaying. He stuck his vines in a different direction, where they didn't bump into anything.

After the auditorium program, everyone gathered in the lobby for milk and dinosaur-shaped cookies. Soon it was time to settle down for the night. Chaperones herded kids in small groups to the restrooms with their toothbrushes. Sleeping bags were unrolled all over the floor of the big dinosaur hall.

Norman and Michael carried their bags into Gallery Six and pulled off their shoes and socks.

The room was darkened now. The only light shone dimly from behind the walls around Dr. Sparks's research plants because now was their daytime.

The cosy glow was like a nightlight. The steggy stood motionless, a huge dark shape in the shadows.

The boys put out their plants' sock dinners and smeared a little orange juice on their curled up leaves. Then they crawled into their sleeping bags.

A chaperone came in to check on them. "Everything OK in here?" she asked. They said yes. "Don't you want to come and listen to the bedtime stories in the big hall?"

"We better not," replied Michael. "We're supposed to sleep here by our plants." She said, "Sweet dreams," and went away.

Norman grumbled, "I wanted to go hear the stories."

"Quit complaining," said Michael. "If you did, you'd fall asleep in the other hall, and I'd have to drag you all the way back here."

"I would not fall asleep there!"

"You would, too. You always fall asleep early."

"Do not!"

"Do too!"

"Do not!"

To shut Norman up, Michael suggested, "Why don't you make up your own story? You got an

A on your alien story for creative writing."
There was no answer from Norman for a long
time. Michael hoped he was making up a story
and keeping it to himself. Or that he had
fallen asleep.

But no such luck. Norman announced, "I'm
making up a poem about a stegosaurus, but I
can't think of what rhymes with it."

Michael said irritably, "Just go with whatever
rhymes with saurus. That'll be easier."

"I can't think of anything," complained Norman. "You have to help me think of something."

To disentangle himself from this project, Michael said impatiently, "Just go through the
alphabet."

"Huh?" said Norman.

"Put every letter in front of aurus and see
which ones turn out to be a word. Like A, aurus,
B, baurus, C, caurus."

"D, daurus," said Norman. "E, eeaurus, F,
faurus, G, gaurus, H, haurus, I, iaurus, J, jaurus.
Are any of those words?"

"Don't ask me," replied Michael. "I don't have
a dictionary in my sleeping bag."

But now Norman's project had got him going.
He couldn't resist. "You could name your stegosaurus Boris," he said. "Or Doris. Or Horace. Or
you could have three of them, and they could live
in a forest." He laughed.

Norman giggled. He exclaimed, "They can all

sing in a chorus. A stegosaurus chorus in a forest!" That sent them both into gales of laughter.

"And," sputtered Michael, "they can drive a Taurus!" After a while, they settled down. It had been a long day. They fell asleep.

Chapter 6

Late that night, the museum was silent. The only sounds were a guard's quiet footsteps or a chaperone turning the pages of a book as she watched over sleeping children in the big dinosaur hall.

In Gallery Six, Norman and Michael slept peacefully. Fluffy and Stanley were chowing down. They ate slowly, schlurping and burping, enjoying their sock meals. A couple of times their vines bumped the large object that had been making odd noises all day. When Stanley finished eating, he began exploring the dinosaur, feeling along its back and tail.

By accident, he found the switch and pulled. The monster started to move. Fluffy was exploring its front end when the mouth opened. One of his vines went into it. The mouth closed. Fluffy tugged. The jaws held firm. The steggy turned its head back, and the end of the vine snapped off in its mouth.

Of course, Fluffy had plenty of vines, and this one would grow back. But perhaps he had some ancient genetic instinct that standing next to a munching plant eater was not a good place to be. Or perhaps he just panicked at having a vine nipped off by a large thing that had suddenly turned unfriendly. Whatever the reason, Fluffy wanted to get the heck out of there.

Trying to drag himself away on his skateboard, he grabbed the railing and pulled. But he just kept bumping into it because it blocked his way. Finally he found the end of the railing near the wall and pulled himself through the narrow gap.

Now on the other side of the railing, he could use it to pull himself away so the large thing couldn't munch him again. He paused to warn Stanley with a tug. Then he reached around looking for Norman. He found him on the floor and felt his face. Norman's nose twitched, but he didn't wake up. Fluffy couldn't find an arm or foot to grab because Norman was cocooned in his sleeping bag. So he twined the tip of a vine around a lock of Norman's hair and yanked.

"Ow!" squawked Norman. Fluffy waved some vines at Norman and then pulled himself along on his way out of the gallery.

Norman looked around, totally bewildered. He saw a flurry of leaves as Fluffy disappeared through the doorway. From the floor he saw the huge steggy looming above him. It raised its head and rolled an eye at him. For one groggy moment, Norman thought the steggy had chomped his hair.

But as the jaws opened, he saw the piece of vine hanging out. He realized why Fluffy was running. Norman wriggled out of his bag.

"Wake up!" he told Michael. "Wake up! The steggy bit Fluffy, and he took off!"

He stuffed his bare feet into his shoes, not stopping to tie the laces. Without waiting to be sure that Michael was following, he ran off in the direction Fluffy had taken—into the dark, deserted galleries that lay beyond.

The sound of the dinosaur also startled Michael. That wasn't supposed to be happening. The meaning of Norman's words began to sink in. He sat up. How had the steggy gotten turned on? Norman and Fluffy were gone. Stanley was frantically trying to get outside the railing. What was going on? Then he noticed the vine hanging from the monster's jaws. It dawned on him that Stanley was trying to get away from a plant eater. No wonder Fluffy had run.

Michael rolled his plant from behind the railing to the middle of the room, a safe distance from the steggy.

"Don't worry," he told Stanley. "It can't get you here. I'll be right back."

As he dashed off after Norman, he thought:

What am I saying? There's no danger from a fake dinosaur—not unless it falls over on top of you. It crossed his mind that maybe he should go find a guard or chaperone. But catching Fluffy was something he and Norman should be able to take care of quickly. No point in getting other people in an uproar. Fluffy couldn't be far ahead of them.

"Norman," he called softly. He felt his way carefully along in the dark. There was no answer.

Two galleries ahead of him, Norman was calling softly, "Fluffy, where are you? Rustle your leaves, so I can find you. Or try to burp." Silence. He moved on, feeling his way along a wall of glass cases.

Far ahead of Norman, Fluffy dragged himself from the last gallery on that end of the building. He rolled into a short hall and bumped into a wall. He felt around all over the wall but found nothing to grab onto to move himself. But he did find a small round spot that moved a little at the touch of a vine. He pressed harder. The wall slid open.

Fluffy reached inside and found a railing across the back of a little room. He pulled himself in. The wall slid shut behind him. Feeling safe from the dinosaur at last, Fluffy relaxed, hidden in the elevator.

Norman came almost as far as the elevator. He stopped because he noticed a thin beam of light down a hall to his left. He turned that way and found the light was coming from a door slightly ajar.

He recognized the NO ADMITTANCE sign. This was the door to the hall where Joe had taken them to his department. Norman was surprised that the door was unlocked. But since it was open, maybe Fluffy had gotten through here somehow. Pushing the door open, he tripped over something. Ever the neatness nut, he picked it up. It was a magazine like the ones in Joe's office. Farther down this hall he saw another beam of light from another slightly open door. Maybe Joe was in there and could help him find Fluffy.

As Norman started down the hall, the door swung closed behind him. He hadn't realized that the rolled-up magazine had been propping it open. The lock clicked.

Moments later, Michael passed by on the other side of the locked door. He recognized it as the way to Joe's department, but he knew it took a key to get through. So there was no chance Fluffy and Norman had gone that way. He hurried on.

Back in Gallery Six, when the steggy started up again, Stanley pulled himself close to the little plants. He reached out to rescue them from the plant eater. A couple apparently took this to mean he wanted to arm wrestle. But Stanley was bigger and stronger. He jerked all six off their platform and plunked them on the floor.

Since they were not on skateboards, he gripped them firmly with six of his vines and used the rest to pull himself out of the gallery, dragging the little ones behind.

Norman pushed open Joe's department door. He was in such a hurry that he didn't see another magazine propping it open. He tripped over the magazine, accidentally kicking it into the room. Behind him, the door swung shut. The lock clicked. Norman tried to open it. He was locked in.

Perhaps someone else might have been thrilled to be locked in with a bunch of millions-of-years-old fossils. But Norman just wanted to find Fluffy. He had to get out of here. But how? He remembered the phone on Joe's desk and ran into the office.

Norman sat in Joe's desk chair and surveyed the messy heaps. The phone was in there some-where. He soon found it under the top layer of stuff. He pointed a finger to press the number to call Dad and Mom. But he didn't know the Sparkses' number.

He knew how to look up numbers in a phone book, but he couldn't find a phone book. So he did the next thing that crossed his mind. He called 911.

A calm woman's voice answered, "911. What is your emergency?"

"I'm locked up in the paleo part of the Natural History Museum, and I can't get out."

"You're what?"

Norman repeated his problem.

She asked, "Are you sick or injured?"

"No."

"Are you in any danger?"

"No, just locked in. I was following my plant because he was running away because a fake dinosaur tried to eat him."

The woman replied patiently, "Let me speak to your mother or father or babysitter."

"They're not here."

"They left you home alone?"

"No! They're at the Sparkses' house. I'm in the Natural History Museum. In a really messy office. And I can't get out."

"You should be in bed asleep at this time of night, not making prank calls."

"This is *not* a prank call. And I *was* asleep. Next to my brother and the dinosaur that attacked my plant."

The woman warned, "We tape all these calls. And we're going to have to contact your parents. On my computer screen I've got the number you're calling from and the address and . . . oh, my goodness! You really are calling from one of the offices in the museum. Keep calm. We'll get in touch with a night guard there. Since you're not in any danger, you can hang up now. I'll call the guard office again in a few minutes to be sure they found you."

Norman hung up. While he waited, he couldn't resist straightening up Joe's desk. He started sorting out the papers by size—big ones in one pile, middle-sized ones in another, and little ones in a third. Under a sandwich wrapper, he found some old dried-up french fries that looked like they had turned into fossils. When he pulled some pictures out to start another stack, something jingled. He uncovered a ring of keys. One of them must be the key to get out. While he was waiting, he might as well try them.

In the outer room, the fourth key he tried worked on the door to the hall. He was so glad to be free that he dashed out into the hall without thinking. The door swung shut behind him, cutting off the light. Now he was locked in the hall. In the total darkness, Norman couldn't see to try keys on either door. But it would be OK. The guards would be coming to get him any minute. He sat down to wait.

Chapter 7

Michael had found an unlocked door that opened into a lighted hallway.

"Hello?" he called. "Anybody here?"

Out of a door down the hall dashed Joe, with a coffee mug in his hand. "What's the matter?" he asked. Michael explained.

"I'll call a guard," said Joe. Michael followed him back into the room, which had a refrigerator, a coffee maker, and a soft drink machine. On the phone, Joe relayed the news.

"We'll start at this side of the building and meet you in the middle," he told the guard. He grabbed a flashlight from a wall bracket and a walkie-talkie from a drawer.

"Come on," he told Michael. "Hector said to be as quiet as possible. We don't want to wake up all the kids."

Back into dark galleries they went. Joe flashed

his light into every corner of each room. Startling sights appeared in the flashlight beam—a snarling tiger, a coiled python, a dazzling glitter of gemstones, a life-sized family of cave dwellers.

The walkie-talkie beeped. Joe held it so they could both hear. "We found the plant in Gallery 11," reported Hector's voice, "but no sign of the kid so far."

Michael was glad Joe knew how to get to Gallery 11 because he had no idea where they were or in which direction they were going.

When they got there, the plant Hector had captured turned out to be Stanley, who was still clutching the six little plants he had dragged along.

Hector said, "We always have amazing things in this museum, but I've never seen a traveling plant taking other plants for a walk before. It wasn't hard to find them. They left a trail of lost pots and dirt."

Michael said, "This isn't the plant that's lost!"

"There's another one running loose?" Hector asked.

"And my brother, too," added Michael. "He was chasing it."

Hector said, "He couldn't have gotten out of the building. Or into the locked area on this floor."

"Er-uh," said Joe. "We better check the locked area."

"Oh?" said Hector. A beep from the walkie-talkie interrupted them. Hector repeated the message: "The police just called. The kid's locked in the paleobotany office. He called 911."

He looked at Joe sternly. "Did you prop those doors open again because you didn't have your keys handy? How many times have all us guards told you to stop doing that?"

Joe explained, "I just went to get some coffee. I'd propped the doors open earlier in case my kids woke up and wanted to find me. But I didn't think anyone else might be wandering around. And I was coming back in a few minutes. I just didn't stop to hunt for my keys."

Hector said, "What you need is a rope so you can hang those keys around your neck! Come on, let's get the kid."

They set off at a fast walk. Michael called back to Stanley, "Stay there! I'll be back in a few minutes!" Stanley tried to follow but found he wasn't going anywhere. Hector had handcuffed his main stalk to a railing.

They found Norman sitting on the floor in the dark, patiently waiting since he knew someone was coming to let him out.

"Are you all right?" Michael asked, putting an arm around his brother.

"Yeah," replied Norman, "Did you find Fluffy?"

"He's not with you?"

"I couldn't find him. He disappeared!"

Hector radioed in: "One lost kid located and

secured. One large plant still on the loose." Unlocking the door to Joe's department, he reminded him, "Get your keys."

They waited while he walked into his office.

"Oh, no!" they heard him howl. They rushed in after him.

"What's wrong?" asked Hector.

"Vandalism!" exclaimed Joe. "Somebody cleaned up my desk!" He turned to glare at Norman.

Michael stepped in front of his brother and said, "He can't help it. He's a born neatness nut. He didn't mean any harm."

Norman reminded Joe, "You said if I cleaned up the environment I could start with your desk."

"I was kidding!" shouted Joe, throwing up his hands. "OK, I'm sorry I exploded. Maybe it won't take me too long to get things back to normal." He looked over the desk. "Did you find my keys?"

Norman dug them out of his pocket and handed them over.

"I found those magazines you lost by the doors," he said helpfully. "I put them in a pile with the ones on your desk. And I put your fossil french fries in the middle drawer with the pens and pencils."

Joe clapped a hand to his forehead but did not reply.

Hector said, "Let's go." They set out again in search of Fluffy.

In the elevator, Fluffy had found more round spots that moved slightly at a touch. He pushed. The little room sank to the basement. The doors opened. There was nothing for his vines to grab onto to pull himself out. But Fluffy didn't want to get out. He was happy riding in his little room. The doors closed. Up he went, and down again, doors opening and closing. Up, down, up, down.

Around the corner from the elevator, Hector whispered, "Shh! I think I heard the elevator opening. Who's there?" he called. They heard the doors close. No one answered. Whoever it was would have to pass where they could see. But no one came. They heard no footsteps. When they got to the elevator, they had passed no one.

"Nobody should be coming or going from the basement at this hour," said Hector. He radioed to get another guard for backup while they checked the basement.

Norman suggested, "Maybe there's a Phantom of the Museum that kidnapped Fluffy and took him inside the walls to a secret room."

"Sorry to disappoint your vivid imagination," said Hector. "There's no such thing except in stories. Come on." He led them back around the corner in their original direction.

As Norman started to follow, he glanced back at the elevator. The doors opened. There was Fluffy!

"Oh!" said Norman. He ran into the elevator to get Fluffy out. As he got behind the plant to push, the doors closed. Fluffy had already pressed B for basement. Down they went.

Michael, Joe, and Hector ran back around the corner. Norman had vanished.

"He must have taken the elevator to the basement," said Hector. "But why? And why did he say 'Oh!' "

The first thought that crossed Michael's mind was that a Phantom *had* grabbed him. He said, "Norman wouldn't go down in a spooky basement by himself in the middle of the night on purpose."

Joe said, "Maybe he thought it needed cleaning up."

Hector punched the button to call the elevator back up.

When the doors opened in the basement, Norman shoved his plant out with a mighty push. He called, "Hey! I found Fluffy!" No one replied. By the light from the open elevator, he noticed that this wasn't where he got on.

"Uh-oh," he told Fluffy. The doors closed, leaving them in the dark. He fumbled around to find the elevator button.

Upstairs, the doors opened on the empty elevator. "Do we have to wait for the other guard?" asked Michael.

Hector said, "He'll be here any minute. I'll tell him we've gone down." While he radioed this message, the doors closed. Hector pushed the button again, but the doors didn't open.

Down below, Norman was glad to see the lighted elevator reopen. As he shoved Fluffy in, one of his untied shoes slipped off. When he turned back to find it, the doors closed on Fluffy, leaving Norman behind. He pounded on the doors in the dark. "Fluffy!" he yelled. "Come back!"

Upstairs, as they heard the elevator begin to open, Hector said, "Here he comes now." He was surprised to see the large plant instead of Norman.

"Hey, Fluffy!" said Michael. "Where have you been?" He stepped inside and behind the plant to help Norman roll it out. But Norman wasn't there. Michael gave Fluffy a hard shove. The plant sailed out on its skateboard. Fluffy had already pressed B again, so the doors closed and Michael was gone.

Joe told Hector, "This is like a magic show. Every time the magic box opens, something different disappears or shows up."

The magic box opened one more time, producing both boys.

"Come out here!" commanded Hector. He stuck his foot between the doors to keep them from closing.

They went back to Gallery 11 to unhandcuff Stanley and put the smaller plants back in their pots. Then Hector made the boys and all the plants spend the rest of the night locked in the guard room.

In the morning, breakfast was served in the lobby. Hector and Joe had given Norman and Michael strict orders not to leave their plants alone, so they took them along. When no one was looking, Norman sneaked a little orange juice to Fluffy.

Michael took Stanley with him to the gift shop to buy the fossil he had looked at yesterday. As he waited for a salesperson to get it out of a glass display case, he didn't notice that Stanley had decided to go shopping, too.

He checked the fossil's twelve-dollar price tag and turned to the nearby checkout counter. The cashier punched a lot of cash register keys and announced, "That'll be forty-seven dollars and fifty-two cents."

"But this fossil only costs twelve dollars," he protested.

"Yes," she said, "but the seven pairs of dinosaur socks are four dollars apiece, plus sales tax."

"What socks?" he asked, bewildered.

"Those," replied the cashier, pointing at Stanley. The plant had seven pairs of dinosaur socks sticking out of various parts of his greenery.

"No," said Michael. "I'm not buying these. It's

a mistake." He began prying the socks from Stanley's clutches and putting them back on the nearby sock shelves.

"Uh-huh," said the cashier suspiciously. She looked as if she thought he was trying to shoplift by smuggling socks out in a plant. Michael felt his ears getting hot with embarrassment. And Stanley wouldn't let go of the seventh pair of dino socks. Michael wondered why he was so determined to have them.

He counted all his money and saw that he could afford one pair in addition to the fossil. The cashier refigured the total.

"Do you want a bag for that?" she asked.

"Just for the fossil," he replied, because Stanley wouldn't let go of the socks. He wished he could get a bag big enough to put completely over Stanley.

When Mom and Dad came to pick the boys up, she asked, "Did you have a good time?"

Norman yawned. "We were up mostly all night," he said. "The steggy bit Fluffy and Fluffy took off and I followed him and Michael followed me and Fluffy disappeared and I got locked in the paleo office so I called 911 and everybody came and got me out. Joe got mad 'cause I cleaned up his desk really nice. But we couldn't find Fluffy 'cause he was like the Phantom of the Museum going up and down in the elevator. And Stanley rescued Dr. Sparks's plants from the steggy." He paused for another yawn.

Michael added, "But besides all that, we had a good time."

Dad picked up their sleeping bags. "Hurry up and roll the plants back to the gallery. We have to get going to the dig. Max is coming along. His sniffles have cleared up. Susan's students will plantsit until we come back at six to pick up Stanley and Fluffy."

Michael said, "There's one little problem."

"What?"

"We have to take the plants with us. After last night, the museum wants them to leave now."

Mom remarked, "I was looking forward to a day without plants."

They loaded Stanley and Fluffy into the RV and drove away.

Chapter 8

On the way to the dig, they drove a long way on back roads. Michael tried to catch up on some lost sleep. But he kept waking up because Norman babbled most of the way, giving Max, Mom, and Dad a play-by-play account of his night in the museum.

Finally, they came to a bunch of cars and vans parked on the edge of a field. "This must be it," said Dad. When they got out of the RV, they saw people off in the distance at the bottom of a small cliff. As they walked toward the group, Joe waved. He introduced them to some of the others. They were inspecting a large area of fallen rocks.

Joe explained, "The winter frosts and thaws and rains bring down rock falls. That exposes surfaces that couldn't be seen before." He led them to the cliff wall and pointed out the wide and narrow layers of rock it was made of. "Like a big cake with many layers," he said.

Michael laughed. "That's the biggest cake I've ever seen," he said.

Joe said, "There are lots of bigger ones—mountain ranges, the Grand Canyon, deep valleys—all over the world. Even under the oceans."

Apparently Joe didn't want to turn Norman and Max loose with hammers because he assigned them to look at all the little rocks scattered over one area. He showed Michael and Dad how to use hammers to split larger flat rocks open along narrow edges to see if any fossils were inside.

"What are we going to find?" asked Michael.

"I don't know," said Joe. "Sometimes we don't find anything. Sometimes wonderful things." Michael hoped they would find something wonderful today. He settled down to work with the hammer.

Mom stayed only long enough to look around and decide that she didn't want to spend the day grubbing around on her knees and pounding rocks. "I'm going back to the RV and read a book," she announced. "I'll enjoy having some time to myself. See you later."

Norman's and Max's attention spans ran out about every two minutes. They kept picking up stones and running over to Joe to ask, "Is this anything?" They took turns complaining: "We're not finding anything. Why aren't we finding anything? When are we going to find something?"

Dad asked Norman, "When are you going to stop whining?"

Norman replied, "If I stop whining, then will we find something?"

"Why don't you and Max go back to the RV and keep Mom company?"

"No," said Norman. "We want to find something."

"Ask Mom to give you a snack," Dad insisted.

"OK," said Norman. He and Max strolled away toward the RV parked far off by the road.

Now that Norman and Max had taken their whining elsewhere, the main sounds were the clink-clink-clink of hammers. Michael also heard rocks splitting and murmurs of conversation from the other searchers. Because he worked leaning over, his sunglasses kept sliding down his nose. He picked up another flat rock, braced it on edge with his knee, and whacked it with his hammer. It fell open. The inside of the two halves was blank. No fossil. He reached for another one to try. He hadn't known that archeology could be such hard work and so boring.

Mom gave Max and Norman apple slices and crackers with peanut butter. She went back to reading her book.

Norman told her, "I need to take Fluffy outside for sunshine. He didn't get any yesterday, or today either."

"His top is getting sun by sticking out of the roof," she said, not looking up.

"If he gets more sunshine, he won't eat so many socks tonight," he reminded her.

"Oh, all right. But don't wander off back to the dig and leave Fluffy alone out there." She helped them take the plant outside.

The boys sat on the ground to finish their crackers. Mom had wrapped them in paper towels so they could put them in their pockets. After a while, Norman asked, "What do you want to do now?"

"I don't know," said Max.

Norman folded up his empty paper towel and put it in his pocket. Max copied him.

"Let's look around here," said Norman. "Maybe we can find something."

Max pointed out, "The ground over there has little bumps. Maybe those are something."

But the little bumps turned out to be just dried mud that crumbled at the scuff of a sneaker. Norman realized that they were wandering away from Fluffy. He walked back to bring the plant along on their stroll. They went on, pausing to scuff more mud bumps.

"Maybe we can find one that doesn't fall apart, and it'll be something," said Norman. They walked on, keeping their eyes on the ground. They scuffed every bump along the way.

Norman said, "Maybe there's something buried under where we're walking right now. Like a whole giant dinosaur."

"The biggest dinosaur in the world," said Max. "Big as a skyscraper!"

"That would be great!" said Norman. "We'll be famous discoverers! We'll be rich! We'll be on TV!" He stopped walking. "But first we have to find it." He dropped to his knees to feel the ground. "Ouch!" He moved one knee to see what was poking it. It was a hard little bump. It didn't crumble. He started clawing at the dirt. "It's something!" he shouted. "I think I found something!"

"Let me see!" said Max. "What is it?"

"It's a bone! A little dinosaur bone!" He kept digging. "Here's another one next to it!"

"Be careful," warned Max. "Don't break it! We should get Joe." They turned around to see which way to go to get back to where the others were. They had wandered a long way.

Norman said, "I'll go get him and Dad. You and Fluffy guard the bones!" He took off running. When he got halfway back to the others, he yelled, "Bones! We found bones!"

Dad and Joe ran toward him and followed him back. Max showed them their find.

Joe smiled. "I'm not an expert on dinosaur bones, but I do know what these are."

Norman asked excitedly, "From a baby steggy? Or a duck-billed thing?"

"What you have here," said Joe, "are chicken bones."

Norman asked hopefully, "From a prehistoric chicken?"

"No," replied Joe. "Probably from a Kentucky Fried Chicken. It looks like some hiker ate lunch here not long ago."

"Rats!" said Norman.

Dad told him, "I know you're disappointed, but at least you two found something. The rest of us haven't found anything so far."

Norman and Max looked cheered up. "I'm taking the bones home," Norman said. Then he handed one to Max. Norman wrapped his in the paper towel, "in case of germs," he said, and put it in his pocket. Max grinned and did the same.

Dad said, "I thought you were at the RV. Didn't Mom tell you not to wander off?"

"She told us not to wander off and leave Fluffy alone. So I took him along."

"That's not what she meant," said Dad. "Take him back to the RV. Then either stay there, or come on back to where we're working. No wandering. OK?"

"OK," agreed Norman. As Joe and Dad walked away, he scuffed the dirt with his shoe and looked around.

"We better get going," said Max. Norman started pushing Fluffy. About halfway back to the RV, Fluffy hit a bumpy spot and started to tip over. Norman threw himself between Fluffy and the ground and went sprawling. His plant put a vine under his arm to help him up. Fluffy also brushed the back of Norman's jeans and jacket to get the loose dirt off.

Max said, "I wish my plant could do things like that. All it can do is eat bugs."

With another vine, Fluffy was feeling around on the ground to find that bump he had hit. He tapped Norman on the shoulder and back of the neck. Norman thought the plant was trying to tickle him.

"Stop it," said Norman. But the plant wouldn't stop.

Max said, "Fluffy looks like he's pointing. At a big bump." Norman got down and clawed at the dirt.

"It's another bone!" he said.

"Another chicken?" asked Max.

"It's smaller," said Norman. He pulled the one from his pocket to compare. Max took his out and put it next to the new one, too.

Norman said, "It doesn't look the same. But this could be from a different part of a chicken."

"I like wings," said Max. "With barbecue sauce. That doesn't look like wing bones."

Norman put the new one in his pocket. "I'm keeping it for my bone collection anyway."

"No fair," complained Max. "You got two, and I only got one!"

"My plant found it," said Norman huffily, "so I get to keep it."

Max did not reply. They trudged on silently for a little way. Norman started to feel bad about hurting his friend's feelings. But he didn't want to give up the bone. "Let's try to find another one," he suggested. "Then we'll be even."

He thought that if they didn't find one more, then maybe he would chop the new bone in half and give part to Max. Or if they found a bigger one, he would keep that and give Max the smaller one.

They got down on their knees to search for more bone bumps. Fluffy brushed at the dirt in several places and then pointed at one spot. Norman dug there. He pried a little bone loose and found two more under it. He put the biggest one in his pocket and handed Max the other two.

"Now we're even," he said.

Max replied happily, "We got enough chicken bones. Let's go get some more peanut butter crackers."

Back at the dig site, Joe found a stone with small leaves in it. Dad found a fern fossil. Michael kept searching, Every time he broke a rock open, he hoped that he would discover something ancient inside. But he kept on finding nothing.

He tried one more, and one more, and one more. Then, to his astonishment, the next one he broke open revealed in its two halves perfect impressions of a large rolled-up leaf, part of a vine, and a couple of flat leaves. They looked like Stanley's and Fluffy's leaves, only a little bigger. His yell brought everyone running.

Joe exclaimed, "This is like the Asian fossils! It's an ancestor of your plants!" He got a magnifying lens from his backpack and peered through it. "Look at that!" he said, handing the lens to Michael. He pointed to a small mass inside the rolled-up leaf. "This is astonishing!" he said.

"What is it?" asked Michael.

"An insect," said Joe. "A partly digested one."

Michael said, "This plant was eating a bug?"

"Looks like it," said Joe. "And meat-eating plants from this era are unknown. This is a sensational find."

Michael asked, "Do you suppose it ate this kind of bug to get nutrition it needed, like other meat-eating plants do?"

"Possibly," replied Joe. "But I'll have to get some entomologists—insect experts—to help with research on this."

Michael wondered if this bug had the same nutrition to these ancient plants as socks did to Stanley and Fluffy. He said, "Maybe this old plant ate bugs because there weren't any prehistoric socks. Do you know where I can get some of these bugs to see if our plants would like to eat them?"

Joe said, "You can't get these anywhere. They're extinct. But maybe they have some modern relatives you could try."

At the end of the day, Mom and Dad invited Joe and his children to stay for dinner in the RV. Norman and Max showed Joe's sons the chicken bones they had found. Joe glanced at them.

"Wait a minute," he said. "Where did you find these other ones?"

"Out there somewhere," said Norman. "I don't know exactly. Fluffy found where to dig."

Joe said, "These others aren't chicken bones. They're from a baby hadrosaur. We have to find the spot where you got these."

They left the rest of their dinner uneaten and fanned out to find the place. Finally, by following the faint traces of skateboard tracks where the boys had walked with Fluffy, they came to the right place. Joe marked the spot. "We'll come back to search this area," he said.

Norman and Max were disappointed when Joe told them they couldn't keep the dinosaur bones. He explained that the deal with the land owners was that any fossils found here would belong to the museum.

Joe said, "Of course, you can take your chicken bones home to show your friends."

Chapter 9

Before they left the Sparkses' to go home Sunday evening, Mom told Dad, "We forgot to call home to see if there were any messages on the answering machine."

"I'll do it," said Dad.

Mom said, "I don't think there'll be any messages. I told everybody who might call us that we'd be away."

Dad made the call, listened, and said, "Oh, no!"

"What's wrong?" asked Mom.

"Norman rerecorded the answering message."

"A different one?"

"No, the same one."

"There's nothing wrong with that," said Mom.

"He sang it to the tune of 'Camptown Races.' So anybody who called while we've been away got a short concert."

"Maybe nobody called. Are there any messages?"

"I can't punch in the code to play them back until Norman stops singing."

There was one message. When Dad heard it, he exclaimed, "Oh, no! The botanical garden called. One of the plants we sold them is causing big problems. It's out of control. The director says we have to do something about it."

"Do what?" asked Mom.

"He just said we'd better take care of it, unless we want a lawsuit."

"They might sue us?" she said, looking worried.

"I hope not," he replied.

Dr. Sparks, who knew the director, offered to call him the next day to see if there was anything she could do. But she suggested, "It's only about a six-hour drive from here to the botanical garden. Michael and Norman have always managed to control Stanley and Fluffy very well. Maybe they can figure out what to do about this other one. Why don't you stay here tonight and go there in the morning?"

"It's worth a try," agreed Dad.

The next morning Dad called the botanical garden director, Mr. Maple, to let him know they were coming. He wasn't in his office, so Dad left a message that they were on the way. He also called his boss, the RV rental place, the boys' school, and Mrs. Smith to let them know they wouldn't be home for one more day.

Six hours later, when their RV pulled through

the gate of the botanical garden, Michael thought it was one of the most beautiful places he'd ever seen. The drive wound through vast spaces with trees, shrubs, a lake, walking paths, and benches.

They came to a large cluster of buildings, some with glass-paned roofs and walls. They found a space in the parking lot. Mom said she would stay in the RV with the plants.

Inside, a guard at a reception desk called Mr. Maple, who hurried out to meet them.

"Thank goodness you've come!" he exclaimed. "Is that your RV in the lot?" Dad nodded. "You're parked right under my office window. I saw the tops of those magnificent specimens through their plastic coverings. How wonderful of you to bring us two replacement plants. We'll only need one, of course, but we'll keep them both for a few weeks to see which one works out best. I'm glad we won't have to sue you. You've solved our problem! I'll have the other plant dug up and put in a container so you can take it away with you now."

"No!" said Norman.

"Wait a minute!" said Michael.

Dad said, "They're not replacements," but Mr. Maple was already dashing away. "Come along!" he called before they could explain further.

Into a large greenhouse they went. "This is our desert environment," explained Mr. Maple as he hurried along. "For plants that live in dry climates."

Michael wanted to stop and look at the amazing cactuses, but Mr. Maple rushed on. In the next greenhouse the air was hot and moist. Going in felt like getting swatted in the face with a wet washcloth.

"Rainforest," said Mr. Maple, waving an arm at the dense greenery. They heard dripping water and smelled damp earth.

In the next section he stopped for a moment. "This is our prehistoric garden," he said, "for plants that lived in the time of the dinosaurs. School groups love this." He led them past the cycads, ferns, and other plants around a pool. Since these were planted in the ground instead of in containers like the ones in the museum, they were big.

Mr. Maple said with a smile, "We tell the children to pretend that a little dinosaur may be hiding behind the ferns and peeking out at them."

Norman told him, "You should get one of those real electric ones. Kids would like that. But be sure not to get a plant eater. The plants would all leave."

But Mr. Maple was moving on, not listening.

Michael muttered to Norman, "These plants don't have skateboards, so they couldn't go anywhere even if they wanted to."

Norman replied, "They *should* have skateboards, just in case."

Mr. Maple finally stopped to unlock a door and

86

held it open for them to enter. The room was dark until he switched on a dim light. In the center of the large room stood Stanley's evil twin—Jason's plant. It was a little shorter than Stanley and Fluffy, but bushier.

Mr. Maple explained, "We've changed their light cycles so we'll have them eating socks in two shifts during the day. That way we can sell more tickets, instead of having them both eat at the same time. The other one is very well behaved. It eats between eleven in the morning and noon. This one was supposed to eat between one and two."

Going over to take a close look, Dad asked, "So what's the problem? It won't eat on time?"

"Don't get too close," warned Mr. Maple. Dad stepped back.

"Uh-oh," said Michael to Norman.

"Things were going fine with training this one," explained Mr. Maple. "And then disaster!"

Norman whispered to Michael, "I bet he's not singing to it or talking to it."

"It started tripping staff members with its vines," said Mr. Maple. "At first we thought it was accidental. Then we realized it was doing it on purpose. So we all began staying out of its reach. Then it began throwing things."

"What kind of things?" asked Michael.

"First, socks—throwing them at us instead of eating them. That was irritating, but harmless.

One day it grabbed a watering hose and gave itself a shower. We thought that was funny and would be entertaining for visitors to see. But a few days later, it started swinging the hose around like a weapon, knocking equipment over. And two days ago, just before I gave up and called you, it picked up a bag of fertilizer, squashed it until it burst, and spewed fertilizer all over me and two other botanists. That was the last straw!"

Michael remembered how Norman had tamed down Jason's plant after Jason neglected it and then stopped feeding it. That had made the plant furious. He wondered what had happened now to send it into tantrums here.

Norman must have been wondering the same thing, because he asked Mr. Maple, "What flavor socks did it throw?"

"Flavor?" asked Mr. Maple, looking puzzled.

Michael said, "He means what colors."

"Lots of different colors," replied Mr. Maple. "Why do you ask?"

Michael explained, "This plant especially likes white socks with brown stripes. Maybe it lost its temper because it didn't like the other colors. And were the socks dirty?"

"Huh?" responded Mr. Maple.

"This plant was grown from a seed from my plant that eats dirty socks. So that's probably the kind it wants—dirty fudge ripple. I mean, dirty white ones with brown stripes. Somebody has to wear them first 'til they get a little smelly."

Mr. Maple said, "Thank goodness this isn't my problem anymore, now that you've come to take the plant away. I'll have someone move it out to your RV and bring the other two inside. If both the replacements work out, we'll pay you for the second one. With three plants, we could sell even more tickets every day."

Dad said, "I'm sorry, but we're not handing over my sons' plants. Let me explain."

Mr. Maple cut him off. "I don't want to get unpleasant about this, but if you don't give us a replacement for this plant, we'll have to turn the matter over to our lawyers. I don't think you want a lawsuit over this."

Dad said, "We'll give you your money back for it. Then we'll be even."

"That won't work," said Mr. Maple. "We've spent a lot more than just what we paid you. We've outfitted a special display area with a new lighting system. Botanists have worked around the clock to train the plants to eat during the day. We've bought signs and printed brochures. We announced that we're going to have two amazing plants, not one. We've sold thousands of dollars worth of tickets in advance. So giving our purchase price back won't do. We have to have another plant that behaves itself and eats socks on schedule to entertain and educate the public. And we're opening this exhibit in three weeks!"

Norman shouted, "You can't have our plants!" He ran over to the troublesome plant and started stroking its leaves.

"Get away from there!" yelled Mr. Maple. "You'll get hurt!"

"He won't hurt me," said Norman. "He knows I'm a friend. Remember me?" he asked the plant. "I used to visit you in back of Jason's garage and talk and sing to you." The plant lashed out with a vine, grabbing Norman's arm. But Norman didn't flinch. He just started singing, "Oh, Susanna" slightly off-key. The plant relaxed, let go, and patted him on the head.

"See?" said Norman. "You just have to treat him nice and sing."

"Sing?" said Mr. Maple. "You're kidding!"

"No," said Norman. " 'Oh, Susanna' and 'Camptown Races' are good. Maybe try the Hokey Pokey, too."

While Norman sang, Michael sat down and quickly took off his socks. Fortunately, he was wearing the right flavor. He approached slowly and dangled one sock in front of the evil twin. The plant perked up, suddenly alert, sensing the delicious aroma of sweaty feet. Then, whap! It snatched the sock from Michael's fingers and sucked it in with a hearty "Schlurrrp!"

"See?" he told Mr. Maple. "Dirty fudge ripple works every time. Try it!" He offered him the second sock.

Mr. Maple took it and edged slowly toward the unruly plant. "Hello," he said. "I'm your friend, too. OK? I have another tasty sock for you." He paused before getting within reach of the vines to see how the plant might react. The plant replied to his friendly words with a very loud burp. He hesitated.

Norman reminded him, "Don't forget to sing." He started on "Oh, Susanna" again. Mr. Maple joined in. This odd duet seemed to calm the evil twin. It plucked the sock from Mr. Maple's hand and ate it. Schlurrp!

Dad suggested cheerfully, "See? If you and your people will just talk and sing to it and feed it dirty fudge ripple socks, that should solve the problems." He began backing toward the door, motioning to the boys to come along.

"It apparently does work!" exclaimed Mr. Maple. He stood close to the plant, talking and singing to it. "We are friends now, aren't we?" he told it. The plant responded with another burp.

Behind his back, as he was busy singing to the plant, Dad and the boys quietly left the room. Then they took off running back through the prehistoric garden, the rainforest, and the desert. Reaching the lobby, they slowed to a walk.

Norman said, "Maybe we should go back and tell him about the ancient plants eating bugs. Maybe the evil twin would like bugs."

"Keep moving," muttered Dad.

As they passed the guard at the desk, trying to look casual, Dad remarked to him, "We left Mr. Maple in with the troublesome plant. He's got it under control now."

Outside, they ran for the RV.

Dad pushed the boys in the side door of the RV and yelled to Mom, "Drive!" She started the engine and headed out of the parking lot. Michael looked out a window. "Nobody's following us!" he reported.

"What on earth did you do in there?" asked Mom.

Norman said, "That guy wanted to keep Fluffy and Stanley, but we showed him how to get the evil twin to act nice."

Dad explained and added, "We left him singing 'Oh, Susanna' to the plant." Mom laughed. She began singing the song. They all joined in. Stanley and Fluffy waved their vines in time to the music. Michael put on another pair of socks to get them smelled up in time for Stanley's late-night dinner.

After they got on the interstate highway, Norman looked out the window and asked, "Where are we going now?"

"Home," said Mom. "Thank goodness."

Chapter 10

Back at home, when Michael was unpacking, he wondered what to do with the dinosaur socks Stanley had forced him to buy. They were too expensive to feed to the plants, and they looked too goofy to wear. Only Norman would wear socks like this. But he already had a pair.

Even so, maybe he could trade these to Norman for something good later. He tossed them into the dresser drawer where he kept his socks and forgot about them.

Norman asked Dad about whether he and Mom had decided about a greenhouse yet.

"Not yet," said Dad. "For the time being we're going to continue to go broke slowly buying socks."

Norman suggested, "We could experiment with

Fluffy and Stanley to get them to eat something else."

Mom said, "Unless it's something really cheap, don't even think about it."

Mrs. Smith came over with a computer print-out three and a half feet long. "Here's the whole schedule for the wedding," she said. "I marked your parts with yellow highlighter."

Mom remarked, "You really have this well organized."

Michael looked over the schedule. It started with picking up people at the airport and taking them to motels, arranging flowers, running errands, and fixing food. Dad was on the list for setting up tables and chairs in the church meeting hall for the reception. Mom was listed with the rolls. Michael found his name next to "Bring birdseed bags in a basket with you to church. Leave under table inside front door during ceremony. During 15 minutes for taking pictures of bride and groom and attendants, get bags out and give them to guests waiting outside church door."

Following that were: "Bride and groom exit church front door." "Guests throw birdseed." "Everybody go next door to church hall for reception."

Norman's instructions were in the reception part: "Fill Water Blaster with syrup. When we are ready to cut wedding cake, bring Blaster to that table. Stand next to person serving frozen yogurt. Ask each person if they want chocolate syrup. Before squirting, aim very, very carefully."

"Everybody eat cake and yogurt," the schedule continued. "Then everybody talk, dance, and have a good time. Before bride and groom leave, bride throws bouquet."

When Norman saw this, he said, "Why is she throwing her bouquet away? She shouldn't be littering."

Mom explained, "She's not throwing it away. It's a tradition at weddings. The bride throws her bouquet up in the air. All her unmarried women friends try to catch it. The one who does, the custom says, will be the next one to get married."

Norman wondered, "Why doesn't she just hand it to the one who wants to get married next? Why does she throw it?"

"So all the women can have a chance at catching it."

"Then the one who catches it gets married?" he asked.

"Not necessarily," said Mom. "It's not a sure thing. It's just a nice old superstition. It's not really true."

Norman said, "Shawn should throw a bouquet to his friends, too."

"Why?"

"Then the girlfriend who catches Belinda's bouquet could marry the boyfriend who catches

Shawn's bouquet. That way she'd have somebody to marry for sure."

Mom said, "Only the bride gets to throw a bouquet."

"But why?" persisted Norman.

"I don't know," said Mom. "The next time you go to the library, get your father to help you look it up."

Norman said, "There's an awful lot of throwing things at a wedding. Bouquets. Birdseed. Can I take my baseball? Bob and I can play catch in case we get bored."

"No," said Mom. "That's final. Over and out."

The boys started their birdseed-bagging assignment, sitting on a sheet of plastic on the kitchen floor to catch the many seed spills. After three days of working on it after school, they were almost done.

The night before the wedding they finished up. The kitchen smelled wonderful from the rolls Mom was baking. Wearing jeans and a sweatshirt dusted with flour, she was clumping around in her new green high-heeled shoes.

"I'm breaking them in," she explained, "so they'll feel more comfortable when I wear them tomorrow." She sat down, took off one shoe, and rubbed her toes. "Well, at least they'll look good," she said.

Dad scrubbed out Norman's Blaster with detergent and hot water. He wrapped it in plastic to keep it clean until it was filled with syrup the next day.

Norman signaled to Michael to come to their room and closed the door. He whispered, "I got a surprise."

"What is it?"

"It's sort of an experiment. A surprise for Mom and Dad."

"What is it?"

"Promise you won't tell until we see if the experiment works?"

"OK."

"Cross your heart and hope to die?"

"Yes!" snarled Michael. "What is it?"

Norman put his ear against the door to be sure Mom and Dad were not out there.

Then he whispered, "Bugs by mail."

"What!"

"I got bugs by mail. I thought maybe Fluffy and Stanley could eat those instead of so many socks."

"How could you order bugs by mail without Mom and Dad knowing?"

"Mrs. Smith was busy, so I got Bob's mom to do it with her credit card. That way they send them by fast mail right away. I told her it was a surprise for Mom and Dad."

"Oh, boy," said Michael. "It's a good thing you told me in time. This could have been another disaster. Did they come yet?"

"Nope. Maybe tomorrow."

"Are they being delivered here?"

"No, over at Bob's. I'm paying his mom from my saved up allowance money."

Norman was disappointed at Michael's lack of enthusiasm for his great experiment idea. He added, "If we could get them to like bugs, then we won't have to go broke buying socks or a greenhouse."

Michael asked, "Do bugs cost less than socks?"

"I didn't figure all that out yet."

"Well, as long as you're already getting the bugs," said Michael, "we might as well try a couple of them and see what happens."

"I hope it works," said Norman.

The next morning, Dad and the boys went over to the church meeting hall to deliver the rolls and help set up for the reception. Michael helped Shawn carry in many pots of Mrs. Smith's prize-winning African violets in full bloom for center-pieces for the tables. They set up twenty round tables and put eight chairs around each one. The tablecloths turned out to be too long and came all the way down to the floor. But it was too late to get shorter ones. Then they set up the big, long tables for serving food.

Mrs. Smith hurried over to Dad. "We have a small problem," she said. "My uncle was bringing two potted palms for greenery for the church altar. Then we were going to move them to the reception to make a nice setting for the cake table. He just called. His van broke down, so he's getting a ride with my sister. But there's no room in the car for the palms. Could we borrow your big plants?"

"Uh," said Dad, trying to think of a good excuse.

"Thanks," said Mrs. Smith. "I really appreciate this. I know they look a little weird, but they'll be better than nothing." She hurried off.

Michael told Dad, "It'll be OK. They hardly ever act up in the daytime."

"You better be right," said Dad.

Mom wasn't happy to hear that the plants were going to the wedding.

When she calmed down, Dad said, "It's a nice day out, and the church is only six blocks away. Do you want to walk over with the boys and the plants?"

"Not in these shoes," she said. "You go with them. I'll drive and bring the basket full of birdseed bags."

The church was beautifully decorated with flowers. Stanley and Fluffy stood on opposite sides of the altar. Shawn stood next to Fluffy. He looked nervous but happy.

Just before Belinda came down the aisle, Michael heard some people in the pew behind him whispering, "What kind of plants are those?"

In the pew in front of him sat their neighbors, Mr. and Mrs. Kramer, their daughters, Mary and Ashley, and their toddler son, Kyle, who wiggled during the whole ceremony. His mother kept shushing him.

After Belinda and Shawn pledged their vows, they came down the aisle arm in arm, looking very happy. Mrs. Smith was crying and smiling at the same time.

Dad and Norman hurried to roll the plants over to the meeting hall and load up the Blaster.

Chapter 11

Michael stood outside the church door handing out the little bags of birdseed. People milled around on the sidewalk, waiting for the bride and groom to come out. He had a few bags left when Kyle strutted up to him and asked, "What dat?"

"Birdseed," said Michael.

"Bood seed," repeated Kyle, reaching out for some.

"No," said Michael. "You might put it in your mouth." He turned away.

"BOOD SEED!" demanded Kyle, stamping his feet. "BOOD SEED! BOOD SEED!"

To shut him up, Michael handed him a bag. "But don't put it in your mouth! OK?"

Kyle nodded and grinned. Mrs. Kramer caught up with him. She untied Kyle's bag and poured some seed into each of his tiny hands. "Don't let go until Belinda and Shawn get here. Hold on tight. And don't put it in your mouth. Here they come! Now throw! Throw!"

Everyone else threw seeds up into the air to rain down on the happy couple. Kyle threw his straight ahead, all over Michael's knees. Seeds pattered down onto Michael's shoes. Some got stuck in his shoelaces.

Kyle raised his little hands to Michael. "Aw gone," he said. "Mo bood seed!" Michael slipped the leftover bags into his jacket pockets and showed Kyle his empty hands. "No more," he said. "I'm saving the rest for the boods."

Mrs. Smith came up behind him. "We didn't invite anyone named Bood," she said. "So you don't have to save any for them." She hurried along.

The church hall looked beautiful. Large African violets and candles stood on every table. Even the too-long tablecloths looked good. Stanley and Fluffy stood calmly like tall sentinels at opposite ends of the table that held the magnificent three-tiered wedding cake.

As guests entered, they walked in a line to hug or shake hands with Belinda and Shawn and their relatives.

Michael and Norman went along with Mom and Dad to the canape table. They helped themselves to punch and filled their plates with fruit, cheese, tiny pizzas, and other little goodies.

"Save room for the main course," called Mrs. Smith as she dashed by.

When they sat down at a table, Mr. and Mrs. Kramer, Ashley, and Mary came and sat in the other four chairs. Kyle sat on his mother's lap to eat.

The main course was chicken with mixed vegetables, salad, and Mom's delicious rolls. Then it was time for the dessert. Shawn and Belinda went to cut the cake. Cameras flashed and people clapped.

Norman stood at the end of the dessert table, in front of Fluffy. He handled his loaded Blaster very, very carefully. First, people picked up a slice of cake and a scoop of frozen yogurt. Those who wanted syrup paused for a Blaster squirt.

When Belinda stood in front of him and held out her plate in front of her beautiful white dress, Norman warned, "Stand back." His aim was perfect, right on the yogurt. As others filed past, he pumped out syrup perfectly. No drips, no squiggles, no chocolate puddles. People smiled and chuckled at this unusual way of serving syrup. When the syrup ran out, Norman refilled the Blaster.

After Michael got his dessert, he walked around the plants, just checking. Everything was fine with Stanley and Fluffy. He went back to sit at the table. The Kramers had gone to get cake.

Mom had asked Dad to go get a plate of dessert

for her, too. "These shoes are killing me," she explained.

"Take them off," said Dad. "The tablecloth is so long, no one will see."

She slipped them off and said, "Ahhh, that feels better."

The band started playing, and the bride and groom had the first dance. Then other couples got up to dance.

When Norman's syrup-squirting duties were over, he came back to the table with his own plate of dessert.

Michael said, "Where did you leave the Blaster?"

"On the table with the yogurt in case anybody wants some more."

"Some little kids might pick it up," advised Michael. "You better put it somewhere where nobody can mess with it."

Michael left to go to the men's room. Norman got up to get the Blaster. When he came back to the table with it, Mom and Dad didn't see him because they had turned around to talk to some old friends standing next to them. Norman slipped the Blaster under the table where no one could see it. It would be safe there.

Mr. Kramer came back and sat down. As they were all talking, he said suddenly, "Oh, sorry. I didn't mean to step on your feet, whosever they were."

"Not mine," said Dad.

Mom figured he must have stepped on her shoes, but she didn't want to point out that her feet weren't in them. She assured him, "That's all right. I didn't even feel it."

So none of them realized that what Mr. Kramer had actually stepped on was Norman's Blaster.

Mrs. Smith came by and persuaded Norman to dance with Ashley Kramer. As they stepped back and forth in one spot on the dance floor, she exclaimed, "Aren't they adorable?"

Norman liked to dance by himself, but dancing with a girl, holding hands, was something he hadn't done before. From the expression on his face, anyone could see he wasn't liking it. Ashley seemed to be enjoying it a lot.

Mr. Kramer went off to get his wife to dance.

Dad said to Mom, "Let's dance." Thinking of her uncomfortable shoes, she looked reluctant. "Just one dance," he coaxed. "Come on."

Mom felt around with her toes, found her shoes, and shoved her feet into them.

"EEE-YEW!" she exclaimed, scrooching her mouth up as if she had just bitten into a lemon. "There's goo in my shoe!" She pulled her feet out from under the tablecloth. Brown goo oozed out around her right foot.

"Oh, no," said Dad. "Not again." He looked under the tablecloth and saw the Blaster. Mom saw it, too.

She yelled, "Norman!" But he had already heard her howl about goo in her shoe and had ducked under a nearby empty table to figure out what to do next. The long cloth hid him completely.

Mrs. Smith came running over. "Let's go to the ladies room," she told Mom. "I'll help you clean up."

With one shoe on and her gooey shoe off, Mom hobbled toward the ladies room, leaving a trail of chocolate footprints.

Dad went looking for Norman. When he didn't find him, he came back and looked under the table to get the Blaster to put it in a safe place. But the Blaster was gone.

Chapter 12

Mary Kramer had been assigned to watch her little brother while her parents had a dance together. She'd been playing a game of "Where's Kyle?" with him to keep him happy. He would duck behind things. She would say, "Where's Kyle," pretending not to see him. Kyle would pop out, grinning, and Mary would exclaim, "There he is!" Kyle would laugh and run on to find another hiding place.

But when Kyle lifted a tablecloth and found the Blaster, he lost interest in the "Where's Kyle?" game. He clutched it upside down, trying to figure out how to make it work.

"Put that back where you got it," commanded Mary. Kyle shook his head. When she stepped toward him to take it away, Kyle dropped the Blaster on the floor. He raised his hands to show he was giving up.

"Come on," said Mary, ready to unload Kyle on someone else. "Let's go find Mommy and Daddy."

But Kyle didn't want to go find Mommy and Daddy just then. He jumped on the Blaster, landing with both feet. Splat! A blast of chocolate hit Mary's ankles and began oozing onto her good shoes.

"You slimed me!" howled Mary. Kyle ran away with his sister in hot pursuit.

Mrs. Smith came over to see what had happened. She picked up the Blaster and shoved it back under the table to get it safely out of the way.

Soon after that, Mom and Dad came back to their table. When they sat down, Mom's foot bumped into something underneath. She looked. "Here it is," she said. "We'd better lock this in the car trunk until we're ready to go home."

"I'll do it," said Dad. "See if you can find the boys. I haven't seen them lately."

Mom looked in the direction of the plants on the far side of the room. The boys were not there.

As Dad turned to leave with Blaster in hand, a man he knew from work and his wife stopped by their table to say hello. Dad put the Blaster down on a chair so he wouldn't look like an idiot standing there holding it. Mom stood up, too, and nudged it to make sure it was no longer pointing at her.

As they all chatted, she stood with her weight

on one foot, with her other knee slightly bent. She didn't notice Kyle, who had led his sister on a chase around the room and was now coming towards Mom off to the side. When Kyle looked back to see if Mary was gaining on him, he didn't notice Mom, either. When he ran into her, they both wobbled off balance. Kyle managed to stay standing, but Mom went backwards and sat down hard on the chair holding the Blaster.

With a mighty spurt, chocolate syrup burst forth all over Kyle. He shrieked, turned, and ran. Everyone who saw him coming got out of his way, but Belinda was facing the other direction. He ran into her and left a Kyle-shaped chocolate smear on the back of the skirt of her beautiful white dress.

Belinda tried to look behind her. "What was that?" she said.

Shawn explained and said, "Don't sit down."

Mrs. Kramer caught up with Kyle. She took a cloth from an empty table and wrapped him in it to carry him out without getting gooed up herself. By now Kyle was calmly licking syrup off his fingers.

Mom went along with Belinda to the ladies room to get the chocolate off her dress.

Unnoticed, beside the deserted cake table, Fluffy was dipping a vine into the punch bowl, touching the melting edges of the floating orange sherbet. He raised the dripping vine to one of his ice-cream-cone-shaped leaves and let the sherbet drip-drip-drip into it.

Michael was moving around the room, avoiding Mrs. Smith. She was on the lookout for children she could get to dance together. As he passed an empty table, he heard Norman whisper, "Psst! Psst! Don't turn around. Don't let anybody see you looking!"

"What are you doing behind the table?" whispered Michael.

"I'm not behind it. I'm under it. I'm waiting for Mom to calm down."

Michael tried to talk quietly without moving his lips. "Ashley's looking for you, too. She wants to dance again."

"Then I'm stuck here," said Norman. The table rose a little on one side, moved a few inches, and went down again.

"Ooops," said Norman.

This gave Michael an idea. "Try to move the whole table over to the door. Then you can duck out into the hall and nobody will see you leave."

Norman tried, but he started going the wrong way.

"Wait. Don't you know how to do anything?" said Michael impatiently. "I'll show you." Looking around to make sure no one was watching, he strolled around to the far side of the table. Dropping from view, he lifted the table cloth and crawled under.

He showed Norman how to put his shoulders up against the table top and move it, all scrunched over. He crept along a few steps and stopped. "See? It's easy," he said.

Norman asked, "But what if somebody sees the table move?"

"I'll be the lookout," replied Michael. "Just let me get out of here first." He peeked out from under the tablecloth to see if the coast was clear. But two pairs of feet were walking toward them. The feet stopped right next to the table. Michael motioned to Norman not to move. Now they would have to wait until the people moved away.

Belinda noticed that some of the children who had been persuaded to dance together didn't look like they were having much fun. She stepped up onto the bandstand and whispered to the leader. He announced, "The bride says that now would be a good time to play an old favorite we always do at weddings—one that people of all ages like to dance to."

Belinda and Shawn were rounding up people to form a circle.

"Here we go!" said the leader.

The band played a few familiar notes and the leader began singing: "Put your right hand in, take your right hand out, put your right hand in, and shake it all about."

Under the table, Norman said, "Uh-oh!"

"Uh-oh is right," agreed Michael. "We better move the plants out of here fast." He peeked out again. The feet were still there but pointed away from them.

The table began creeping toward the doorway. Then it went faster as it raised up a little higher so the boys could shuffle faster.

They heard someone say, "Where is that table going?"

"Is it on rollers?" asked someone else, who didn't have a clear view.

"No," said someone else. "It's wearing shoes!"

As soon as the table got to the doorway, it got stuck because it was too wide to go through. That was fine for the boys' getaway. They scrambled out unseen into the hall and ran around to the door on the other side of the hall, where Fluffy and Stanley were.

Fluffy was shaking himself all about in a whirl of vines and splashing in the punch.

Stanley was bopping to the beat, keeping time with his vines. It was an amazing sight, but the people on the dance floor were having such a good time that they didn't notice. And everyone else was watching the dancers and clapping to the music. So when Norman and Michael popped up from behind the cake table and shoved the leafy

112

dancers out the nearest door to the hall, nobody noticed.

"Calm down," Norman told Fluffy. But Fluffy wouldn't stop dancing, although his vines were starting to get gridlocked.

Michael said, "They'll stop when the song stops. At least out here nobody will see them." The boys sat down on the floor by the wall to wait by the Hokey Pokeying plants.

"I hope Mom and Dad didn't notice," said Norman.

Michael replied, "Dad was doing the Hokey Pokey. I didn't see Mom."

"Maybe she's still washing her foot," said Norman.

When the Hokey Pokey was over, the band started playing a slow tune. The plants settled down immediately. Michael wheeled Stanley back in by the cake table and returned to help Norman untangle Fluffy's vines. Then Norman put Fluffy back by the table. The boys sat down on the floor behind the cake table to keep a close eye on the plants, just in case. Mom found them there.

Norman said, "The Blaster disaster wasn't my fault."

"I figured that out," said Mom. "Come back to the table where I can keep an eye on you."

When it was time for Belinda to throw her bouquet, Mrs. Smith rounded up all the unmarried women into the middle of the room. They laughed and waved their hands in the air. Belinda tossed the bouquet high. But she didn't throw it straight. It veered left, past the cake table.

A vine snaked out and snatched it from sight. Stanley had caught the bouquet!

While the women looked around for the vanished flying flowers, Michael wrestled the bouquet from Stanley.

He took it back to Belinda. "Sorry," he said. "It got tangled up with my plant."

She laughed. "I guess I should have practiced ahead of time. I can throw a baseball straight, but I never threw a bouquet before." She backed off and tossed it again. One of her friends jumped high and caught it.

Michael said, "Great jump!"

"She played basketball in high school," said Belinda.

Norman wondered, "Does this mean Stanley's going to get married?"

"Don't worry," replied Belinda. "Catches by plants don't count."

Mrs. Smith rounded up some more children to dance together. Michael escaped, but when he looked at the dance floor, he saw Norman dancing with Ashley and smiling. They were doing the Steggy Stomp.

Chapter 13

Later, when the family got home, Dad remarked, "I knew this was going to be another day we'll never forget."

"We can try," said Mom, rubbing her sore feet.

Michael said, "The food was good."

Norman said, "And the dancing."

"Yeah," said Dad. "It's fun to dance once in a while. We should do that more often."

Mom said, "That's a good idea. As long as I can wear my sneakers and there's no chocolate syrup involved."

"Weddings are fun," said Norman. "Let's go to some more."

"We don't know anyone else who's getting married," Mom told him.

"Yes, we do," he said. "That basketball player who caught the bouquet."

Dad went to check for messages on the answering machine.

Mr. Maple's voice came from the machine: "I wanted to let you know that the troublesome plant is doing fine now. We're going to put 'Oh, Susanna' into the show for an audience sing-a-long. The plant is also responding well to the Hokey Pokey. We hope to work that into the show later for an audience and plant participation number. I'm mailing you an invitation to the opening day of our sock-eating plant show. Hope you can come." Mr. Maple's voice paused. "By the way," he added, "that's a nice touch—answering your phone like that with a song." The machine clicked off.

"A song?" said Mom. She glared at Norman. "Not again," she said.

"Not me," said Norman. "I didn't do it again."

"Oh," said Dad. "When we got home, I forgot to change the message. So it was still Norman singing."

"Great," said Mom. "So everybody who's left us a message this week, too, got Norman's serenade." Norman looked pleased.

"Let's go to the plant show," he said.

"No," said Dad. "We're not driving eleven hours to see a plant eat socks. We can see that anytime we want while relaxing in the comfort of our own home. That is, if you can call living with Stanley and Fluffy relaxing."

Norman asked, "Where are we going to take a trip to next?"

"After this last one," said Mom, "all I want to do is stay home. Possibly for the next few years."

But Norman was not discouraged. "Let's rent the RV again and go to Hawaii."

Michael said scornfully, "We can't drive to Hawaii. It's in the middle of the Pacific Ocean."

"Oh," said Norman. He thought for a moment. "Then let's rent a submarine."

Dad said, "There aren't any submarine rental places listed in the phone book."

"Did you look?" asked Norman.

"No, but I'm sure there aren't any."

"But how do you know if you didn't look?"

"I'm sure," repeated Dad.

"But why don't you look?" whined Norman.

"You look," said Dad. Norman got out the Yellow Pages phone book and started leafing through it. Finally he happened to find the word submarines in an ad.

"Aha!" he exclaimed. "Submarines!" He took the book over to his father and pointed. "There!"

Dad smiled. "This is a restaurant ad," he said. "The submarines they're selling are sandwiches."

Norman looked disappointed. "But why are they called submarines?"

"Because they're shaped like subs," explained Dad. "The next time we go out to eat, I'll buy you one. You'll have your very own submarine—until you eat it all up."

Norman looked cheered up. "But can we still

go to Hawaii?" he asked, leaning his elbows on Dad's knee.

"Why Hawaii?" asked Dad.

Norman's eyes lit up. "So we can see some more of those night plants like Sarah's and Fluffy can learn to dance the hula," he explained.

Mom said, "Let's just borrow some books and videotapes from the library about Hawaii, submarines, and how to hula."

Later, Norman went over to Bob's to see if the bugs had arrived. He returned with a sturdy cardboard box. He hid it in the garage and went to get Michael.

"Did you open it?" asked Michael.

"Not yet."

Michael carefully sliced the sealing tape with a knife and opened the box just a crack to peek in. He half expected a bunch of bugs to come surging out, but nothing happened. He opened it all the way. The box was full of bugs, but they were just lying there.

"They look dead," said Michael. "Maybe the box was out in the cold while they were being sent here. Joe said the cold room at the museum kills bugs."

Norman said, "Maybe they're asleep."

Michael decided, "Maybe Stanley and Fluffy will eat them anyway. We might as well try them tonight."

*   *   *

Just before bedtime, Norman sneaked out to the garage and brought the box of bugs to the boys' room. He put it under his bed until they were ready to experiment.

After Mom and Dad had come in to say goodnight, Norman got out of bed and pulled out the box. He took out a bug and put it in one of Fluffy's rolled-up leaves that the plant used for eating socks. Michael did the same with Stanley.

Then they watched and waited for a long time. The plants made no moves to suck in the bugs.

"Maybe they're just not hungry yet," said Michael. "They usually don't eat until later."

"Let's leave the bugs there," suggested Norman. "Maybe they'll get eaten along with the socks."

Long after the boys fell asleep, Fluffy and Stanley began to stir. Stanley picked up a sock and raised it to his rolled-up leaf. But before he sucked in the sock, he shook the rolled-up leaf to get the bug out. It fell on the floor.

Fluffy didn't notice the bug in his leaf until he started to suck in a fudge ripple sock. Evidently the bug taste disgusted him because he stopped and spit out the unexpected insect.

After the plants finished their usual sock meals, they seemed restless and fidgety. Perhaps they were feeling hungrier than usual because of their busy day at the wedding.

Fluffy quietly pulled open Norman's sock

drawer and poked around inside until he found Norman's dinosaur socks. Stanley grabbed Michael's sock drawer and yanked on it so hard that it flew out and thumped on the floor.

The thud woke the boys. In the dim light coming through the slightly open door to the hall they saw Fluffy eating a dinosaur sock and Stanley waving Michael's pair with two vines.

Norman tried to grab his socks away from Fluffy, but Fluffy won the tug-of-war.

Michael said, "Stanley, no! Those are clean socks. You won't like the taste." But Stanley schlurped them up anyway.

Michael said, "Why are they going after socks in the drawers when they've already had plenty to eat?"

Norman asked, "Why are they going after dinosaur socks? That's not one of their favorite flavors. They never even tasted those before."

Michael said, "Aha! Maybe Stanley and Fluffy are trying to turn the tables. For millions of years, their ancestors had to put up with plant-eating dinosaurs. So they're being dinosaur-eating plants—even though the dinosaurs are only pictures on socks."

Norman chuckled. "Turnabout is fair play," he said.

"Or," added Michael, "maybe they're just starting to need more socks to eat." He put his drawer back in the dresser and got back into bed.

As Norman was falling asleep, he said, "They must have eaten the bugs."

"We'll check it out in the morning," said Michael. "If they didn't eat them, the bugs are probably lying around on the floor somewhere." The boys fell asleep immediately.

But now, after several hours in the warm room, the bugs were waking up. Under Norman's bed, the ones in the box found a crack under the lid to escape through. The two that had fallen on the floor started crawling up the wheels of Fluffy's skateboard. Many more followed. Some began heading for Stanley. Others explored other parts of the room.

Bugs marched up the bedposts. Bugs marched up the walls. Bugs marched up Stanley and Fluffy's main stalks. The plants didn't like this. But these unwelcome visitors were too small to get a grip on with a vine. So, looking as if they were being tickled, the plants wriggled and wiggled, trying to shake off the bugs. They swatted and brushed with whirling vines. Fluffy looked like he was dancing a combination of the Hokey Pokey and the Steggy Stomp.

Michael slept on peacefully until Stanley woke him by swatting a bug that was strolling across Michael's nose.